The DRAGON THIEF

ALSO BY ZETTA ELLIOTT

Dragons in a Bag

The DRAGON THIEF

ZETTA ELLIOTT

ILLUSTRATIONS BY GENEVA B

Random House 🏠 New York

Text copyright © 2019 by Zetta Elliott
Jacket art and interior illustrations copyright © 2019 by Geneva B

All rights reserved. Published in the United States by Random House Children's Books, a division of Penguin Random House LLC, New York.

Random House and the colophon are registered trademarks of Penguin Random House LLC.

Visit us on the Web! rhcbooks.com

Educators and librarians, for a variety of teaching tools, visit us at RHTeachersLibrarians.com

Library of Congress Cataloging-in-Publication Data
Names: Elliott, Zetta, author. | B, Geneva, illustrator.
Title: The dragon thief / Zetta Elliott; illustrations by Geneva B.
Description: First American edition. | New York: Random House, [2019]
Summary: Told in two voices, Jax and Kavita, Kavita's brother Vik, and new friend Kenny try to return the baby dragon to the realm of magic before anything else goes wrong.
Identifiers: LCCN 2018032431 | ISBN 978-1-5247-7049-5 (hardback) | ISBN 978-1-5247-7050-1 (library binding) | ISBN 978-1-5247-7051-8 (ebook)
Subjects: | CYAC: Magic—Fiction. | Dragons—Fiction. | Witches—Fiction. | Apprentices—Fiction. | Stealing—Fiction. | African Americans—Fiction. | Brooklyn (New York, N.Y.)—Fiction.
Classification: LCC PZ7.E45819 Dx 2019 | DDC [Fic]—dc23

Printed in the United States of America
10 9 8 7 6 5 4 3 2 1
First Edition

Random House Children's Books supports the First Amendment and celebrates the right to read.

The DRAGON THIEF

1

KAVITA

"Thief!"

The word whistles through the air and pricks the back of my neck. I turn to find Aunty's black eyes fixed on me. She was snoring loudly when I crept into her room just a moment ago. That gave me the courage to pull a chair over to the mountain of boxes and stuffed plastic bags she keeps in the corner. At the very top of the mound of junk is a wire birdcage that's shaped sort of like the Taj Mahal. I need it—and I need it *now*.

I inch up on my tippy-toes and reach for the birdcage. My other hand sinks into the soft, squishy contents of a yellow plastic bag that's wedged between two boxes. I don't know what's inside the bag, and I don't care. Mummy would never let me keep my room like this, but no one ever criticizes Aunty—Papa won't allow it. She's the oldest person in our family and spends almost every day buried under the heavy, colorful quilt that covers her bed. Sometimes she hums to herself and stares out the window. Other times she watches game shows on the little black-and-white TV that sits next to her bed. Now I see her pointing a wrinkled brown finger at me.

"Thief!"

She says it louder this time. I feel my cheeks burn with shame.

"No, Aunty—I—I . . ." By pressing my hand deeper into the squishy plastic bag, I manage to steady myself and turn all the way around to face her. "I just need to borrow— Whoa!"

I was so close to reaching my prize, but then I lose my balance. I fall off the chair, bounce off the foot of the bed, and land on the floor with a thud. My fall brings down an avalanche of boxes, and so I cover my head with my hands. When I open my eyes, the empty birdcage is rolling on its side next to me.

"Tut-tut-tut." Aunty makes the strange sound without opening her mouth. "What a mess you've made."

"Aunty? Is everything all right?"

My eyes open wide. If Mummy comes upstairs, she'll want to know why I'm in Aunty's room. And if I tell her the truth, she'll want to know why I need an old

birdcage. I can't tell her that there's a dragon in my bedroom. I can't tell anyone that I'm a dragon thief!

Aunty watches me with a slight smile on her face. Against her dark skin, her black eyes sparkle with amusement. I don't think she's angry with me, so I decide to plead for help.

"Please don't tell on me, Aunty! I'll clean everything up—I promise."

We both know Mummy's standing at the foot of the stairs. Her hand is probably on the railing, and she's wondering whether she needs to come upstairs to check on Aunty. My heart is pounding fast and hard, but I don't yet hear Mummy's slippered feet climbing the stairs. "Please, Aunty," I whisper.

Aunty clears her throat and calls, "I'm fine, dear. I just knocked over some boxes. Kavita's here to help me."

We wait, frozen and silent, until we hear Mummy's voice floating upstairs. "Okay, Aunty. I'll be up soon with your lunch."

Because she's an elder, Aunty doesn't have to do much around the house. She really only leaves her room to use the toilet and take two-hour baths. Aunty doesn't even come downstairs to eat with us unless we have company over on special occasions. Mummy brings Aunty's meals up on a tray. I scan the messy room for a clock and find one on the nightstand next to the bed. It's a square digital clock that Vik and I gave to Aunty last Christmas. Its giant blue display reads 11:38.

I hop to my feet and scramble to pick up all the things I've just knocked down. Aunty waves her hand at me and says, "Leave it, child. It makes no difference to me whether they are up against the wall or on the floor. What is it you came to borrow?"

I feel guilty, so I set the chair back on its legs and stack a couple of boxes on its seat. Then I point to the pink wire cage and say, "I came to borrow your birdcage, Aunty."

Her dark eyes narrow as she squints at me. "You don't have a bird."

My cheeks burn again, and I dig my toes into the thick green carpet. "No, Aunty."

After studying me for a moment, she says, "Do you have some other kind of pet?"

I nod without looking up. How much should I tell her?

"I put it in a box, but . . ." I stop and decide not to tell Aunty that the dragon set the cardboard box on fire. "I need something stronger."

Aunty leans back against her pillows and smooths the quilt with her hands. "I see. And your mother doesn't know about this new pet of yours."

It's not a question. I nod again and dare to glance at Aunty's face.

"Then you'd better take it," Aunty says with a nod at the cage on the floor. "I had a songbird once, but I set it free before I left India. I only keep the cage to remind me. . . ."

I pick up the cage and hold it to my chest. "Remind you of what, Aunty?"

She sighs and closes her eyes. "That every living thing wants to be free."

I look down at the cage in my arms. It might be shaped like the Taj Mahal, but it's not a palace and certainly not a good home for a baby dragon. My cheeks burn again, and this time tears spill from my eyes.

"Come here, Kavita," Aunty says.

The kindness in her voice draws me over to the bed. I sit on the edge and sniffle once or twice.

Aunty hands me a tissue, and I set the cage on the floor once more so I can blow my nose.

"You probably want to keep your pet safe," she says softly.

When I nod, Aunty asks, "Do you think it will be happy in this cage?"

I shake my head, and more tears run down my face. "Oh, Aunty!" I sob, throwing myself across the bed. "I've messed everything up. I just wanted one for myself—and Jaxon had three! But I don't know how to take care of it, Aunty. I know it's hungry, but every time I feed it, it grows and grows. . . ."

Aunty strokes my hair and makes that tut-tut-tut sound once more. But this time it's meant to soothe me, not chastise me. "Every problem has a solution," she assures me. "We can figure out what to do if we put our heads together."

I look up from the pillow and blink away my tears. Aunty is smiling at me, her round face framed by tiny, defiant silver curls. I put my arms around her and give her a hug. It feels good knowing I've got someone to help me care for the dragon. I couldn't ask my big brother what to do. Vik would just yell at me for stealing from his best friend.

Aunty hands me another tissue from the box on her nightstand. When I've blown my nose and dried my eyes, she says, "So. Tell me about your new pet."

I open my mouth to tell her just how marvelous the

dragon is but stop when I hear scratching at the door. It creaks open, and a tiny purple head appears. I gasp.

"Oh no—Mo!"

I jump up from the bed. How did the dragon get out of my bedroom? I put it inside the laundry hamper and made sure to close the door behind me. A knot of dread twists in my tummy. The dragon couldn't have burned a hole through the door—could it? I sniff the air but don't smell any smoke.

Aunty grips her quilt and pulls it up close to her chin. "A rat!" she cries.

"No, no, Aunty—it's not a rat. It's . . . a dragon."

Aunty's jaw drops, and her eyes open wide. Then she fumbles for her glasses and takes a closer look at her unusual visitor. The dragon squeezes past the door and cautiously enters the room. I haven't been feeding it, yet the magical creature has grown to be almost as big as a kitten. It even mews and purrs like one! But instead of whiskers and fur, the dragon has metallic scales and triangular plates that run along the ridge of its spine.

"Well, well, well," Aunty says with obvious admiration. "Now I've seen everything!"

Even though the dragon doesn't belong to me, I still feel proud of it. But my smile vanishes when I hear the

soft thud of footsteps coming up the stairs. My eyes dart to the clock. It's noon—time for lunch!

"Uh-oh!" I cry. "Mummy's coming!"

Aunty points at a wicker basket on the dressing table. "Quick," she says, "put your little friend in there!"

I scoop up the writhing dragon, but when I open the basket, it's crammed full of sewing stuff.

Aunty sighs and throws up her hands. "I've been meaning to clean that out. No time now. The waste bin—quick—empty it!"

I do as I'm told, and an avalanche of crumpled-up tissues tumbles onto the carpet.

"Sit—sit!" Aunty hisses.

I trap the dragon under the metal waste bin and sit on it just as Mummy pushes the door open with her back and enters the room with a tray of steaming food.

"I made your favorite, Aunty," Mummy says in the high singsong voice she uses only when she's trying to hide the fact that she's annoyed. "I hope it's to your liking."

Aunty smiles up at Mummy but then looks at the tray of food and wrinkles her nose. She sniffs the fragrant steam rising from the plate and says, "Tut-tut-tut. Too much cumin."

Mummy presses her lips together but doesn't say a word. I can tell she wants to say something, but Aunty is an elder and must be shown respect. Once, I heard Mummy and Papa arguing about Aunty.

"She belongs in a nursing home," Mummy had said.

"She belongs *here*—in *our* home," Papa replied.

"She's not family, Adiv."

"Aunty is more than family," Papa had insisted. "She's looked after me since the day I was born."

"And you've cared for her all these years—you brought her to America. You don't owe her anything more."

"I owe her *everything*, Meera. She's staying—and that's final!"

Papa almost never raises his voice, so it was strange to hear him getting so upset. I never heard my parents arguing about Aunty after that. Papa is the one who wants Aunty to live with us, but Mummy's the one who looks after her.

Suddenly, I feel the metal waste bin growing warm beneath me. The dragon must be trying to burn its way out. I squirm as the bin grows hotter and cough a few times to cover the squeals of displeasure coming from the dragon.

Mummy stares at me for a moment. "I hope you're not bothering Aunty, Kavita."

I frown and shake my head. Why does everyone think I'm such a pest?

"Kavita's keeping me company," Aunty says, drawing away Mummy's attention. "It isn't good to eat alone— bad for digestion. You always make such a lot of food." Aunty pushes the basmati rice around with her fork. "Maybe Kavita can help me eat it all," she says doubtfully.

I smile and nod at Mummy, but she knows there's no way I can eat any of the food on that plate. Aunty likes a *lot* of chili pepper in her food—so much that Mummy has to cook it in separate pots. I think the dragon wants to taste Aunty's super-spicy food, because it starts to whine. I start coughing again to conceal the sound.

Mummy frowns and comes over to press her palm against my forehead. "Are you coming down with a cold?"

"She just needs some tea with plenty of honey and cayenne. Why don't you go back downstairs and put the kettle on, dear?"

Mummy's lips twist a bit before finally turning up into a small, tight smile. "I guess I'd better."

I open my mouth to object, but Mummy holds up her hand to silence me. "Aunty's right. Better to treat your cough now before it develops into a full-blown cold. Why don't you put your pajamas on and climb back into bed."

Mummy has a way of saying things that lets me know she's giving an order, not making a suggestion. I know I should head back to my room, but if I stand up, the dragon may escape from under the waste bin.

Aunty saves me by saying, "I'll keep Kavita with me, dear. She can suck on a lozenge for now. I know I've got some around here somewhere. . . ."

Mummy casts a disdainful glance around the messy bedroom. She smothers a sigh and says to me, "Don't talk Aunty's ear off while she's eating, Kavita. And please bring the tray downstairs once she has finished her lunch. You can drink your tea in the kitchen."

"Yes, Mummy," I say from my perch on the uncomfortably warm waste bin.

As soon as we hear my mother going down the creaky stairs, I jump up and lift the bin off the floor. Mo immediately runs to the bed and uses its sharp talons to climb up the quilt.

"Close the door," Aunty says.

I do as I'm told. Then I lean back against the door and watch as the dragon scampers around the bed, chasing the colorful strips of fabric sewn onto the quilt.

"Come here, child," Aunty says, waving me near.

I swallow hard and walk over to the bed. Mo scrambles up Aunty's long braid and snuggles against the soft, wrinkly skin of her neck.

"You're a long way from home, aren't you?" Aunty says softly. "I am, too." She strokes the dragon's belly and then looks over at me. "Well, child. You'd better tell me everything."

2

JAXON

Ma won't wake up—and it's all my fault.

I had one job—*one job*—and I blew it. I'm probably the worst witch's apprentice ever, but Ma gave me a second chance. We left the realm of magic and came back to Brooklyn to find what I left behind: a baby dragon.

But since we've been back, Ma just hasn't been her usual self. I mean, I've only known her for about a week. At first, I thought she was my grandmother, but she's not—Ma's a witch. She can be kind of cranky, but deep down, Ma's not so bad. In fact, she's pretty cool for an old lady. I was looking forward to learning more about witchy stuff, but that can't happen if Ma won't wake up.

My grandfather knows about magic, too, but he's not here right now. Ma and I left him in the other realm with Sis and L. Roy. Mama agreed we could move in with Ma until our landlord fixes our apartment. But he's the worst landlord ever, so Mama's over there a lot of the time, making sure he does everything the judge ordered him to do. That leaves me alone with Ma in her strange apartment.

At first, she just napped a lot. I'd sit in the chair beside her bed and try to make sense of the strange words she muttered in her sleep. But her naps got longer and longer until finally Ma just stopped getting out of bed. Now she doesn't eat or go to the bathroom. She only woke up once, when she heard us talking about what to do. Mama's friend Afua came over to check on Ma. She's a visiting nurse, and after examining Ma, Afua said her vital signs were good.

"It could just be extreme fatigue," Afua said. "Has she been under a lot of stress lately?"

Mama looked at me, and I looked at the floor. Ma was looking forward to retirement, but she had one last job to complete. I said I'd help her, but then everything went wrong. Now it's up to me to make things right. I asked Afua what we should do if Ma didn't wake up.

"Well, I guess you'll need to call an ambulance and take her to the hospital," Afua said.

All of a sudden, Ma sat up and barked, "No doctors!" before collapsing against her pillows. A few seconds later, she was snoring soundly. And that's how Ma's been for the past couple of days.

I'm on spring break, so I can stay with Ma while Mama's at work. There's not much to do in this apartment. Ma doesn't own a TV, so I spend my days flipping through the many books in Ma's living room. There's a whole wall covered in bookshelves, but so far I haven't found anything about how to break a sleeping spell. I never used to believe those fairy tales, but right now a spell is the only thing I can think of. Why else won't Ma wake up? I kissed Ma's cheek just to see if that might work, but I'm no Prince Charming and Ma's no Sleeping Beauty.

Whenever I have a problem, I call my friend Vik. It's his little sister, Kavita, who stole one of the three dragons I was supposed to deliver. So I called Vik as soon as Ma and I got back from the realm of magic, but Mrs. Patel told me he'd gone to New Jersey with his father to visit relatives. I sure do miss my own dad when stuff like this happens. I just met my granddad a week ago, but he's not here, either. In fairy tales, the hero always has loyal companions who help him complete his quest. Right now it feels like everyone has abandoned me, but I don't have time for a pity party. I've got to come up with a plan!

Ma may not need to eat, but I do. When my stomach starts to growl, I go into the kitchen and look inside the empty fridge. Mama said she'd stop at the store on her way home from work. There's one bottle of root beer left, but I decide to save it for Ma. She'll be thirsty when she wakes up.

Suddenly, I hear a strange clicking sound. It gets louder and faster, until finally I realize that something is scratching at the window. I hurry over and raise the paper blind.

"It's you! You've come back!"

As soon as I open the window, the gray squirrel squeezes into the kitchen and scurries across the floor.

"Wait—where are you going?" I call after her, but it's too late. I rush out of the kitchen and down the hallway in time to see the flash of her bushy tail disappearing into Ma's bedroom.

Oh no! If Mama comes home and sees that I've let a rodent into the house, I'll be in big trouble. Then I remember that Ma was pretty upset the last time this squirrel stopped by. Maybe another unexpected visit will wake her up!

When I reach Ma's room, the squirrel is nowhere to be seen. Then I hear a soft thud and notice that Ma's purse has fallen onto the floor. I pick it up and find the squirrel underneath, sifting through the contents that have spilled onto the gold-colored shag carpet.

The squirrel chatters at me, but I can't understand what she's saying. The only item she doesn't toss aside is the red mint tin that once housed the baby dragons.

That was before Kavita fed them. Once she gave them sweet peda to eat, the dragons started to grow and I had to put them in a sandwich bag instead.

"There's nothing in there," I assure the squirrel. "The dragons are gone."

The squirrel cocks her head, pressing her ear against the tin. Then she holds it out to me and taps the lid with her curved claw.

I'm about to tell her that it's empty, when I remember—it's not! Before we left the realm of magic, Sis gave Ma a gift—a helper. A brilliant red butterfly!

18

Ma put the butterfly in the tin after the bumpy ride back to Brooklyn in the transporter. I sure could use some help right now.

I take the tin from the squirrel. It feels light, but then, butterflies don't weigh very much. The squirrel nods at me and clasps her tiny paws together, waiting for me to release the butterfly. But no matter how hard I try, I can't pry off the lid!

"Maybe she sealed it with a spell," I say.

The squirrel seems to disagree. She shrieks and scampers out of Ma's room. I follow her and find the squirrel scratching her claws against the front door.

"Do you want out?" I ask.

She shakes her head and points at me.

"You want me to go outside?"

The squirrel nods and then races past me, down the dark hallway, and back into the kitchen. By the time I catch up with her, she has squeezed through the window and is once more on the fire escape. She points at me one last time and then scampers onto the branch of a nearby tree and disappears.

I look at the mint tin in my palm. I was wrong—not everyone has abandoned me. Ambrose will know what to do!

3

KAVITA

I tell Aunty all about the day Vik took me to meet his friend at the park, finishing my story with this declaration: "I am *not* a thief, Aunty—honest! I didn't *want* to take the dragon from Jaxon's purse . . . I mean, I knew it was wrong, but . . . I *had* to!"

When tears start rolling down my face, Aunty rubs my back and hands me another tissue from the box on her nightstand. Mo stays on Aunty's lap but dips its head to flick its pink tongue across my hand. I smile at the sweet little dragon.

I blow my nose and add, "I only took Mo because Vikram said it thought I was its mother. I just felt like . . . Mo needed me."

Aunty smiles as if she understands. "Mo is its name?"

I shrug. "That's just what I've been calling it—because it's mauve."

Aunty studies the dragon for a moment. There's wonder and admiration in her eyes. "I never had any children," she says softly. "But I remember how it feels to be needed. No one needs me anymore."

I frown. "That's not true. We need you, Aunty."

She shakes her silver head. "You *love* me—that's different. I know I'm a useless old woman. Why do you think I stay in this room? I can't walk without that contraption"—Aunty nods at the metal walker in a corner of her room—"and would just make a nuisance of myself. It's been a long time since anyone depended on me." The dragon snuggles closer to Aunty, and as she strokes its head, the smile returns to her face.

"You're not useless," I say quietly. "You're helping me right now." I pause to ask, "You won't tell Mummy what I've done, will you?"

Aunty shakes her head and winks at me. "I think we'd better find a way to solve this problem on our own."

I wipe away my tears and nod at Aunty. "We have to give Mo back, don't we?"

Aunty sighs and studies the dragon for a moment. "Well," she says thoughtfully, "that boy you took Mo from seems like he could use some help. Perhaps you and I can find another way to ensure that this creature

21

finds its way home. When you lose your home, you lose a part of yourself. . . ."

I reach out my hand and run my fingertips over Mo's silken scales. "The dragon likes you, Aunty. Do you really think Mo is homesick?"

"Not now, perhaps, but in time this creature will grow. It will look around and wonder where all the other dragons are. It will yearn for a place where it can truly feel at home—it will wonder what it feels like to belong."

My cheeks warm, and I cast a shy glance at Aunty. This is the first time we have spent so much time together. Papa always said that Aunty used to tell the best stories when he was a child. Maybe Aunty will tell me one of her wonderful stories today.

For a little while, we sit in silence with the dragon purring happily between us. Finally, Aunty says, "I wonder . . ."

She speaks so softly that I lean in to hear more clearly. "You wonder . . . what, Aunty?"

After another long pause, Aunty looks at me and asks, "Do you know where I'm from, Kavita?"

That's a strange question. Aunty wouldn't play a trick on me, so I give the most obvious answer. "Sure. Our family's from India, Aunty."

She nods, but her eyes leave mine and roam across

the colorful quilt. "You were born here, in America. I was born and raised in the Karnataka forest."

I don't mean to, but I frown. I'm not sure I've ever seen a photograph of a forest in any of Mummy and Daddy's albums. They both grew up in Mumbai, which is a big, bustling city. Aunty sees the confusion in my face and smiles.

"Haven't you ever wondered why my skin is darker than yours? Or why your hair is straight, but mine is curly?"

"People from India don't all look the same," I insist. Mummy's big sister out in Queens has skin that's much lighter than mine. Mummy says Manju Masi puts bleaching cream on her face and hands at night. That's why the skin on the other parts of her body is so much browner.

"My skin is dark, too," I tell Aunty. I place my hand on top of hers, and she stares at it for a moment. We're almost the same shade of brown, but Aunty's wrinkly skin is a bit darker than mine. I reach up and tug at one of the tightly coiled curls that frame her face. "I wish I had curly hair. Straight hair is boring."

Aunty laughs. "When I was your age, I wished I had straight hair! I wanted to look like all the other girls at school with their sleek, tidy braids swinging back and forth as they walked. At home, in the forest, I stood out as well. My hair was curly, but not curly enough." Aunty sighs. "I never found a place where I fit in."

"Mummy says you can lose yourself if you try too hard to fit in."

Aunty snorts. "Easy for her to say—she didn't grow up in America's 'melting pot.' Do you want to fit in?"

I shrug. "Sometimes I want to be like the other kids at school, but mostly I just want to be myself. I like to read and I'm into dinosaurs. I think Mummy wishes I was more like my cousins. They play with dolls, but I'd rather play with Vikram's microscope."

Aunty nods in a way that tells me she approves. I wonder why I never talked to Aunty like this before. She's a good listener.

"Perhaps one day you'll become a paleontologist," she says. "Your great-grandfather was an entomologist—a scientist who studies insects. Did you know that?"

I shake my head. "What kind of bugs did he study?"

"Ants! That's what brought him to the forest, and that's where he met my mother. You're right, Kavita, our family is from India. We are Gujarati and Hindu, but I am also Siddi."

"City? I thought you grew up in the forest."

"S-i-d-d-i. Siddi. In many ways, we were the same as those who lived in the villages and towns outside the forest. We spoke the same language and wore the same type of clothes. But we were different, too. Our roots were elsewhere. . . . In Africa."

My eyes open wide. "Africa? Are you sure, Aunty?" I've never heard about people from Africa living in India.

"Hundreds of years ago, Portuguese traders crossed the Indian Ocean. They sailed to the continent of Africa looking for things to buy and sell. From Zanzibar they bought spices like cloves and carried them back to India. They also took people—as slaves."

Now my mouth *and* my eyes open wide. "You mean . . . African people were bought and sold *in India*? I thought that only happened here in America."

Aunty gives a grim nod. "Thousands of my people were taken across the ocean. Some call us Habshi, but we were much more than slaves. Some of us were soldiers, fighting in the armies of powerful rulers and serving as their bodyguards. Some Siddis married into royal families, and some ruled in their own right. Still others had special skills."

"Like what?"

"Well, Yakut was a Siddi known for his ability to train

horses. The sultana made Yakut master of the royal stable. And legend says he trained other creatures, too."

"Elephants?" I ask.

Aunty shakes her head and nods in the direction of the birdcage. "Dragons!"

Mo perks up at the mention of the dragon trainer. Aunty rubs her fingertip under the little lizard's chin, and Mo's eyes close.

"Those were the stories Nanima used to tell me while we pieced together a quilt like this one made from scraps and rags and the old saris Ba used to bring home. When I was your age, I worked in the fields with my grandmother. My mother walked ten miles to reach the nearest town. There she had a job cleaning and cooking for a wealthy family. Your family. Your great-grandfather used to walk Ba home sometimes. Nanima would insist that he stay for supper even though we didn't have much to eat. Sometimes we caught small fish in the river. Sometimes we ate ants."

"Ants!"

Aunty laughs. "Your great-grandfather thought they were quite a delicacy, but for us, they were a source of protein. Ba was a wonderful cook. She served the ants on banana leaves with a pepper chutney and rice. And for dessert we had fresh honeycomb. That's what I miss most. . . ."

Aunty closes her eyes and smiles at the memory. The pink tip of her tongue slides across her lips as if there were still honey left to taste.

"And even though there was barely enough to go around, Nanima always made us save some for the dragons of the forest. They like sweet things, you see."

"They sure do," I say, thinking of the way the three dragons devoured my peda.

Aunty sighs and removes her glasses so she can wipe her eyes. Then she puts her glasses back on and gently shakes Mo. The little dragon stirs and looks at us expectantly.

"Enough reminiscing," Aunty says. "We'd better get going."

"Where?" I ask.

Mo dashes back and forth on the bed, eager to embark on a new adventure. I grab hold of the dragon and stroke it to calm it down. Aunty flings back the quilt and swings her legs over the edge of the bed. As usual, she's wearing her lima-bean-green sweat suit. Aunty's never warm enough. We bought her a heavy flannel nightgown and a pair of flannel pajamas, but she prefers her sweat pants. Aunty kicks aside the slippers resting next to her bed and points at a pair of leather sneakers in the closet. "Bring me my shoes."

"Where are we going?" I ask again, stressing the *we* this time.

Aunty stands up and forces her feet into the worn running shoes. "Queens," she says before pushing past me to reach a dresser in the corner of her room. I watch as she opens the top drawer and takes out a sari.

"Put your little friend in its cage. Mo won't like it, but it will have to do for now. We'll cover the cage with a shawl. That should soothe its nerves. My pet bird used to go to sleep when I covered its cage, thinking it was nighttime."

I do as I'm told, and to my surprise, the dragon enters the cage willingly. There's a folded pashmina shawl hanging from Aunty's walker. I drape it over the cage, and after a moment or two, Mo grows still.

"What's in Queens?" I ask Aunty.

"If we're going to send your little friend home, we'll need to consult an expert."

My eyes open wide. "You know a dragon expert?"

Aunty groans a bit as she wraps her sari around her body. I rush over to give her a hand. "Thank you, child," she says, lifting the gold-bordered fabric over her shoulder.

"We don't need a dragon expert," Aunty tells me. "We need someone who can find a way to move between realms. What we need," she says, taking up her purse, "is the very best astrologer. And Bejan is the best of the best."

"How will we get past Mummy?" I ask anxiously.

Aunty looks inside her purse and then winks at me. "I have a plan," she says with a mischievous smile. "Take this tray downstairs and bring up the cordless telephone. Then take Mo downstairs and leave the cage by the front door. Can you do that?"

"Yes, Aunty," I say as I pick up the untouched tray of food. When I get downstairs, Mummy is talking on her cell phone. She's trying to be quiet, but I can tell she's complaining about Aunty. When Mummy hears me set the tray down on the counter, she glances at the uneaten food and grabs hold of her hair as if she's about to rip it out. I scan the kitchen and find the cordless phone on its base for once. When Mummy turns her back to me, I grab the phone and run back upstairs.

Aunty is waiting for me. She holds out her hand, and I pass her the phone before carrying Mo downstairs in the covered cage. I put my coat on and set the cage near the front door. Then I run upstairs once more.

Aunty is standing on the landing.

"You need your walker," I remind her.

Aunty shakes her head and jogs for a few seconds. "I don't need it anymore! Your little friend has given me a burst of energy. I feel like a girl again!"

I smile. Maybe some of Mo's magic has rubbed off on Aunty!

"Ready?" she asks.

"Ready!" I reply.

Aunty takes a red flip phone out of her purse and presses a single button. She must be calling someone on speed dial. Seconds later, the cordless phone rings. Aunty tosses it through the open door of my parents' room. The cordless phone bounces on the floor a couple of times before disappearing under the bed. Aunty pulls me inside her own bedroom and closes the door.

"Kavita? Kavita, please answer the phone," Mummy calls from downstairs. "Kavita?"

Aunty holds a finger up to her lips so I don't reply. Soon we hear Mummy's feet pounding the steps as she hurries upstairs. She's still got her cell phone pressed to her ear. As soon as Mummy enters her room, Aunty ends the call and presses another button on her phone. She must be calling Mummy's cell phone, because I hear her say, "Just a minute, Soniah, I've got another call."

Aunty hangs up and calls the cordless phone once

more. Mummy gives an exasperated groan and drops to her knees to search for the ringing phone. Aunty gives me a gentle push and hisses, "Now—go, go, go!"

I dash downstairs and open the front door. I pick up the cage and look over my shoulder to find Aunty running down the stairs. I've never seen her move so fast! We're down the front steps and on the sidewalk before Mummy realizes what's going on. Aunty whistles and a green taxi pulls up to the curb.

"Quickly—get in! Get in!" Aunty says before squeezing in next to me. She pulls the door shut and tells the driver to take us to Queens. I turn my head and look out the back window. Mummy is standing in the street, a phone in each of her hands. The look on her face makes my stomach do a quick flip.

"I'll make it up to you, Mummy," I whisper as I turn back around. I remember to fasten my seat belt and help Aunty fasten hers, too. Then we both lean back and let out a sigh of relief. When the driver asks for an address, Aunty pulls a folded flyer out of her purse. While she's reading the address out to him, I get a glimpse of a red hand. Lines, symbols, and words have been drawn onto the palm. RESULTS GUARANTEED is printed below a man's smiling brown face.

"Is that your friend?" I ask.

Aunty nods. "I haven't seen Bejan in many, many years. We don't have an appointment, but I'm sure he'll see us."

There's a phone number printed on the flyer. "Maybe we should call him," I suggest.

"No need!" Aunty says with a bright laugh. I see the driver's eyes watching us in the rearview mirror. "Bejan is a psychic," Aunty explains. "He knows we're on our way!"

4

JAXON

I head straight to the park. For the first time this week, I feel hopeful. The April sun is struggling to break through the clouds. I want to shout up at the sky, "You can do it!" but instead I whisper those words to myself. Birds are chirping excitedly, and the buds on the branches give all the trees a soft green glow. I'm not the only one heading to the park. Plenty of families have the same idea, and street vendors dangle treats and toys in front of kids who are happy to be out of school for a week. A man walks by with a cloud of blue and pink cotton candy above his head. Kids race up to him, eager to pluck a bag of colored sugar from his pole.

Mama doesn't let me eat junk food, but my dad used to buy street treats for me. It's been almost two years since he died. I still miss him a lot, and I think about my dad even more when I have a problem I can't solve.

When I used to ask him for advice, Dad would never tell me what I should do. He'd ask me a bunch of questions instead, and answering them helped me realize what my options were. I still had to decide what to do, but things always seemed clearer after talking to my father.

Ambrose will know what to do about Ma. But when I reach the corner of the park with the two guardhouses, the bench Ambrose usually occupies is empty. I wade through a sea of pigeons and take a seat myself. Ambrose moves around—always pushing a grocery cart full of junk—so I might have to wait awhile. The birds crowd around me, hoping for something to eat. Ambrose keeps a bag of birdseed in his cart, but I don't have any food on me. I shoo the pigeons away and try to come up with another plan just in case Ambrose doesn't show up.

I could go over to Vik's house and demand that Kavita hand over the dragon. But then what would I do? I can't get the transporters to work without Ambrose. I could take the dragon back to Ma's apartment, but it needs to go back to the realm of magic. Sis's butterfly might be able to help, but I can't open the tin it's in.

When Ambrose doesn't arrive after half an hour, I decide to head over to Vik's house. Mrs. Patel will know exactly when he's coming back from New Jersey, and maybe I can confront Kavita. I want to make sure *she* knows that *I* know she's a thief!

The flock of pigeons disperses as I walk along the sidewalk, but one bird doesn't seem willing to get out of the way. Unlike the other gray pigeons, this one has black feathers. I try to go around it, but the bird seems determined to stay in my path. I don't want to kick this strange pigeon, so I try to take a giant step over it. To my surprise, the bird twists its head and squawks up at me, "Hey, hey! I'm walkin' here!"

A week ago, a talking pigeon would have freaked me out. But over the past few days, I've encountered a very determined squirrel, actual dinosaurs, a talking rat, and three baby dragons. I'm learning to take it all in stride.

"Sorry," I say to the pigeon. "I guess I wasn't looking where I was going."

The bird shifts to the left so we can walk side by side. It studies me for a moment before asking, "Got a lot on your mind, kid?"

I sigh. "Actually, I do. I have a problem—a big problem." For some reason, it doesn't feel weird confiding in a pigeon. In fact, I'm glad I finally have someone to talk to. "I was hoping my friend Ambrose could help me out. But he's not here. . . ."

The pigeon stops strutting and turns its head to one side so it can peer up at me. "You know Bro?"

I nod, and the pigeon shifts its body so it can inspect me with its other eye. The sun finally peeks out from behind the clouds, and I see the shimmer of purple and green on the bird's black neck.

"Huh," it says finally. "Well, Bro does keep company with some strange folk. What do you need, kid?"

"Advice, mostly," I tell him. "Do you know where Ambrose is?"

A shrill whistle comes from the pigeon's beak. "Long gone."

My heart sinks. "Gone . . . for good?"

The pigeon doesn't really have shoulders, but somehow it still manages to shrug. "Can't say. Last time I saw Bro he was falling apart—literally. He's usually a well-put-together kind of guy, if you know what I mean, but something's gone . . . slipping away . . . draining! That's the word he used. Said he could feel the magic seeping out of this world. In his condition, Bro couldn't afford to stick around, if you catch my drift."

I know exactly what the pigeon means. When I first met Ambrose, I thought he was homeless. He was pushing an overflowing grocery cart, and he was wearing more clothes than anyone I'd ever seen. Then I realized the layers of hats and coats and gloves were a disguise—a way of giving himself a human shape, really. Without all his carefully placed clothes, Bro would be invisible.

"Did he go back to the realm of magic?" I ask.

"I think so. Said he was heading home."

"But I need his help to work the transporter!"

"These two are out of order, kid. Bro had to haul all his stuff over to the far side of the park."

"There's a working transporter over there?" I ask hopefully.

The pigeon shrugs again. "Can't say for sure. All I know is, Bro left a while ago and he hasn't come back."

"This is terrible," I moan before sinking onto a stone bench. "Everything's going wrong."

"You can say that again! We can feel it—all of us. Something's not right. There used to be balance, but now everything's out of whack."

I nod and hold my head in my hands. "It's all my fault."

"Aw, don't beat yourself up, kid."

Suddenly, I have an idea. "Do you know Nate—the rat?"

"Sure, everyone knows Nate. Why?"

"Can you help me find him?"

"Nate's gone underground, kid. But I can get the word out that you're looking for him."

"Thanks! I'm Jax. Nate is friends with my granddad, Trub. Uh . . . do you have a name?"

"Call me Soot, kid. You live nearby?"

I nod. "I'm going to my friend's house right now, but we'll stay close to the park."

"Sounds good," Soot says. "Sands are shifting around here—tread carefully."

"What does that mean?" I ask.

"Watch where you step!" the pigeon squawks.

I look down and narrowly miss stepping in a pile of dog crap. I turn to thank Soot, only to find that the pigeon has flown away. The sun slips behind the clouds once more, but I feel much lighter inside. Vik lives just a few blocks away, so I head down Flatbush Avenue. Then I realize what's up ahead and turn down a side street instead.

I never walk down that block. That's where it happened almost two years ago. That's where my dad lost his life. He was walking home, talking to Mama on his cell phone, when an SUV jumped the curb and ran him down. The news reporter called it a random accident, but it didn't feel random to me. The driver wasn't drunk—he was texting. His license had already been suspended, so he shouldn't have been driving at all. He might not have been aiming for my father, but Dad was the only one who died in the crash. A few more minutes and he would have been home with us, telling us about his day, asking us about ours. But that driver took his eyes off the road, and his truck swerved onto the sidewalk, and my dad never came home again.

If Dad had been shot by a cop, maybe someone would have painted a mural. Maybe there would have been rallies afterward and people would have marched with signs bearing Dad's name. But that's not what happened. Mama doesn't know this, but I watched the accident on the local news channel. They run the same stories hour after hour, and the day after it happened, I just sat in front of the TV watching my dad's final moments. Surveillance cameras show him walking along Flatbush Avenue, his phone pressed to his ear. He looks relaxed, his suit jacket slung over his shoulder because it was warm that spring night. Then the SUV jumps the curb, Dad turns toward it, and that's where the footage stops. They never showed the moment of impact, but Mama told me Dad died instantly. "He didn't suffer," she assured me. Suffering's for the folks left behind.

When I told Mama I wanted to be Ma's apprentice, she thought I believed magic could bring my dad back. Sometimes I dream about seeing him again, but I know I can't turn back time or undo what's been done. Terrible things happen every day in this world, but if magic disappears completely, things might get even worse. My granddad says there are two camps: those who believe magic belongs in its own realm, and those who think the realms should merge. I think magic gives people hope, but it also makes some people afraid. Yet if we don't have a bridge between the two worlds, we'll never have a chance to learn how to get along. That's what I need right now—a bridge that will let me take the last dragon back to its siblings.

I'm so lost in my own thoughts that I've forgotten to follow Soot's advice. Or maybe I'm focusing too much on the sidewalk, because when I finally look up, I'm almost at the Patels' house—and Vik is walking toward me!

"Hey, Jax!" he calls out with a wave.

I break into a run and throw my arms around my

friend. "Vik! I'm so glad you're back. I need your help—again."

Vik loops his arm around my shoulders and says, "That's what friends are for. What's up?"

I sigh and suddenly feel my eyes filling up with tears. So much has happened since the last time I saw Vik. Without saying a word, Vik leads me over to a brownstone, and we plunk down on the bottom step of someone else's stoop. Vik leaves his arm around my shoulders, and after a few deep breaths, I'm ready to tell my best friend about all the trouble caused by his sister—the dragon thief.

When my story ends, Vik doesn't say a word. His lips are pressed together in a thin line, and his nostrils flare angrily as he breathes. I've never seen Vik so upset. He's so mad at his sister right now, Vik looks like he could breathe fire.

Finally, Vik explodes. "Kavita is *such* a brat! I can't believe she took one of your dragons. Actually—I *can* believe it because that's just the kind of pain in the butt she is. I'm so sorry, Jax. I never should have brought her with me to the park that day."

"It's not your fault, Vik. The dragons were my responsibility. Where is your sister now?"

"No one knows, and Mummy's really worried. Kavita ran out of the house around noon with my elderly aunt—she's more like a grandmother, really. Mummy says they jumped into a cab. Papa thinks Aunty is just visiting an old friend out in Queens. We're not sure why Kavita went with her, but that's what she does, you know—she tags along and causes trouble!"

"Do you think she took the dragon with her?" I ask.

"Definitely—she'd never leave something that precious behind. She probably thinks she can hide it from all of us. As if anyone could hide a dragon!"

"Well, in the meantime, maybe you can help me with this." I pull the mint tin from my pocket and show it to Vik.

"You need help with mints?"

I laugh and shake my head. "This is the tin from Ma's purse. She kept the dragons inside it until . . ."

Vik rolls his eyes. "Until my bratty sister opened the tin and fed them. What's inside it now?"

"A butterfly from the realm of magic. I'm pretty sure it's not a regular insect. There were a bunch of them buzzing around Sis—she's the guardian of that realm. When we realized Kavita had stolen one of the dragons, Sis sent us back to Brooklyn with a red butterfly. She

43

said it would help us, but now I can't open the tin. Ma won't wake up, Ambrose has vanished, and I don't know what to do."

"Let me try," Vik says, holding out his hand.

I set the tin in his palm, but like me, he's unable to pry it open.

"Why is it so hot?" Vik asks, tossing the tin back to me.

"I don't know," I tell him. "It wasn't like that a moment ago."

"Maybe something's happening inside," Vik suggests.

I try once more to open the tin, but it's hard to get a grip because the metal is heating up. Vik and I are so busy fussing over the tin that we don't even notice who's coming up the street. By the time we look up, it's too late. Kenny O'Connor, the biggest kid in our class, is looming over us.

5

KAVITA

Aunty was right: putting a shawl over the cage has a calming effect on Mo. The dragon is still and silent for the entire trip from Brooklyn to Queens. When the driver pulls up to the curb, Aunty pays him and we get out of the cab. Someone else hops in right away, and the cab speeds off. The sidewalk is crowded, and people grumble and jostle us as they pass by.

"Where are we, Aunty?" I ask.

"We're in Jackson Heights," she tells me. "Bejan's office is in this building, I think."

A bigger version of the flyer Aunty had in her purse is taped to the door. I take a moment to read the words printed in gold. *Change Your Luck! Find True Love! Increase Your Wealth! Improve Your Health! Remove the Evil Eye!* There's nothing about helping homesick dragons, but I'm sure Aunty knows what she's doing.

Aunty finds her friend's name on the intercom and presses the button three times. When we hear the buzz of the door unlocking, we go inside the building and climb a narrow flight of stairs. There is only one empty seat in the tiny waiting room. Aunty tells me to sit down and then nods somewhat apologetically to the other customers before knocking on the closed door. An elderly man answers the door wearing an annoyed look.

"I'm with a client," he says, but when he realizes it's Aunty, a huge smile spreads across his face.

"Nira! I had a feeling our paths would cross today. I'll be with you in just a moment—wait right here."

A moment later, the door opens again, and Bejan pushes an unhappy woman out of his office. "I have an emergency that requires my immediate attention, Mrs. Singh. If you'll just take a seat . . ."

"There are no seats!" Mrs. Singh complains.

I jump up and offer her mine. "You can sit here," I say, moving over to stand next to Aunty.

"Wonderful!" Bejan says. Then he bows to his other customers. "Thank you all for your patience. I'll be with you momentarily."

He opens the door to his office and ushers me and Aunty inside. Once the door is closed behind us, Bejan claps his hands. I jump, and Mo utters a squeal of surprise.

"So—what have you brought me, Nira?"

"You mean you don't already know?" Aunty says with a sly smile. She takes one of the seats facing Bejan's desk and points at the other. I slip onto the chair and hold the cage tightly in my arms. When Aunty nods at me, I remove the shawl. Bejan's eyebrows go up, but he shows no other sign of surprise.

"Well!" he says at last. "I knew something extraordinary was coming my way today, and you have certainly delivered, Nira. People often bring their pets to my office, but I have yet to see a dragon in a birdcage. You can release the creature—it will be safe here."

I check with Aunty, and when she nods, I open the cage door. Mo pokes its head out, sniffs the air, and then scrambles from the cage to my knees and up onto Bejan's desk.

Aunty and I watch as Mo examines the crystals and tarot cards arranged neatly on the desktop. When the dragon reaches for a bowl of chalky pink mints, I quickly snatch it away. Bejan sits perfectly still, a slight smile on his lips. Mo rises up on its haunches, sniffs in Bejan's direction, and then drops onto all fours and creeps a bit closer. Bejan's hands are resting on the edge of his desk, palms down. Now he flips one hand so that the palm is facing upward. Mo looks back at me and Aunty, then inches forward and places one of its paws on top of the astrologer's palm. For a moment, they simply gaze at each other. When Bejan is sure the little dragon trusts him, he takes his other hand and gently turns Mo's paw in order to read the lines there.

"Hmmm," Bejan moans softly. Whatever he sees in Mo's palm must be very interesting.

After another minute of *oohs* and *aahs*, Aunty grows impatient and says, "Bejan—what do you see?"

"This creature is extraordinary!"

I want to say, "Duh—it's a dragon!" But that would be disrespectful. So instead I ask, "What makes Mo so special?"

"I see in this creature's life line the most magnificent destiny. But in order to fulfill its role, it will have to overcome many barriers—and betrayals."

I look at Aunty. She nods at Bejan as if he's making total sense. I'm not so sure. How could he tell all that just from looking at Mo's palm? I wonder what Bejan would see if he looked at my palm.

"Jyotisha, or the science of light, involves the study of the stars and planets. Timing is very important, and you have come to me at just the right time. I will do my best to help you, but in order to perform an accurate reading, I need to know the exact date and time this creature was born."

Aunty looks at me. "Do you know when Mo was born?"

I shake my head. "But I can find out. May I borrow your phone, Aunty?"

She nods and reaches into her purse for the red flip phone. I open it and call my brother. I know he's going to be angry with me, so I take a deep breath and brace myself.

"Hello? Who is this?"

I press the button that puts our call on speakerphone so everyone in the room can hear. "It's me, Vikram. I'm calling you on Aunty's phone. I need some information." The words rush out quickly because I know Vikram will stop listening once he realizes it's me. Sure enough, a second later he starts yelling into the phone.

"Kavita—do you know how much trouble you've caused? You're a thief! I'm going to tell Mummy and Papa, and they're going to ground you FOR LIFE! You better bring that dragon home RIGHT NOW!"

I try to stay calm, but before I know it, I'm yelling at Vikram, too. "Don't tell me what to do, Vikram! This is all *your* fault—*you* said the dragons thought I was their mother. I'm taking good care of Mo. Aunty and I even came to Queens so we can send the dragon home!"

"What? Kavita, don't do anything to that dragon! You've already made enough of a mess."

I open my mouth to yell something else at my brother, but Aunty plucks her phone from my hand. "Vikram? This is Aunty. I realize you are upset, but I need you to listen carefully. We are with an astrologer right now. He is trying to help us, but we need to know the date and time of the dragon's birth. Can you get that information for me?"

Vikram sounds like he's checking with someone else—probably Jaxon. After a short pause, he comes back on the line with the information we need. Aunty scribbles down the date and time on a notepad provided by Bejan.

Aunty switches off the speaker and holds the phone up to her ear. "Thank you, Vikram. Yes, yes—I know all about it. You don't need to yell. Kavita is very sorry for all the bother she's caused. We're doing our best to make things right. . . . Hmm? No, I'm afraid we can't do that. Calm down, child! I'll let you know when we're ready to come home. I have to go now. Goodbye, Vikram."

Aunty snaps her phone shut even though it's clear

that Vikram had more to say. She slides the notepad over to Bejan. He nods solemnly and says, "Now we can proceed.

"There is a tower—a tall structure that marks the gate between worlds. It is not open yet but will be in a few hours' time, when the new moon shines overhead. You must go back to Brooklyn and wait for the gate to open."

"Brooklyn's a big place," I remind him. "How will we find this tower?"

"I will write down the coordinates," Bejan says. "You must take the creature to this location today before the sun sets. Otherwise the new moon will wane and this rare opportunity will be lost. The planets wait for no man, no woman, no child." Bejan's dark eyes rest on me. "In order to benefit from this auspicious alignment, you must act deliberately, with purpose and precision. Do you understand?"

I nod and try to coax Mo back inside the cage. But the little dragon wriggles out of my hands and drops to the floor. It disappears beneath Bejan's desk, forcing me to get down on my hands and knees. I peer under the desk and find Mo clutching something in its paws. It's hard to see in the shadows, but I can tell the dragon is licking the round object.

51

"Mo—no!" I cry.

I lie flat on my stomach and reach for the dragon. It's so busy devouring the lint-covered mint that it doesn't even try to resist. But when I pull Mo out from under the desk and try to pluck the candy from its paws, Mo hisses at me.

"Tut-tut-tut," says Aunty with a disapproving glare.

"Mo must be hungry," I explain. "I know I am."

"Put your friend back in the cage and we'll be on our way." Aunty holds out her hand. Bejan grasps it, pulls her close, and kisses her on both cheeks. Aunty beams at him. "Bejan, it's been a pleasure, as always."

Bejan turns over Aunty's hand and examines her palm, but only for a few seconds. He glances at me, and I think I see sadness in his eyes. Then he smiles at Aunty and folds both his hands around hers. "My friend, I wish you a safe journey. May you find the peace you seek."

That seems like a strange thing to say. Aunty's lower lip trembles, and her eyes start to shine. Before I can ask her what's wrong, she hustles me through the waiting room and down the stairs that lead back to the street.

6

JAXON

Kenny O'Connor is huge. He doesn't say much in class, but then, he doesn't have to. Everyone stays out of his way. Rumor has it he got left back not once but twice. That would explain why he's a foot taller than the rest of us and twice as wide.

Vik and I see Kenny on the bus sometimes, though most days his mom drops him off at school. We've never really spoken before, but now Kenny nods at us as if we're pals. When he flicks his shaggy brown hair aside, I see that his blue eyes are fixed on the red mint tin. I quickly shove it into my pocket and glance nervously at Vik.

"H-hey, Kenny," Vik stammers. "What's up?"

Kenny shrugs and jams his giant fists into the bottom pockets of his vest. It's the kind fishermen wear and could probably fit an adult. That's how big Kenny is.

"Not much," he says finally.

I hear the curiosity in his voice. Why would a kid like Kenny O'Connor take an interest in my tin? Vik looks at me, and I try to think of something else to say— something that will make Kenny go away.

I get up from the stoop and carefully step around Kenny. "Uh . . . we were just heading to the library. We're working on a project."

Vik nods eagerly and jumps up to stand beside me. We could make a run for it if we had to. Kenny's big, but I don't think he's that fast.

Kenny frowns. "For school?"

I nod, but Vik shakes his head at the same time. One of Kenny's eyebrows goes up. Now he's suspicious.

"What's in that little red box?" he asks.

"What box?" Vik asks innocently.

Kenny pulls his hands out of his pockets and folds his arms across his broad chest. "I saw you two fighting over it. What's inside?"

"Nothing important," I say. "It's just an old mint tin." I pull the tin from my pocket and shake it. "See? Empty."

Kenny's eyes shift from my face to Vik's. He unfolds his thick arms and holds out his hand. "Give it here. I can get that lid off."

"Uh . . . that's okay. You probably have more important things to do."

I nudge Vik so he knows to follow me as I start heading up the block. But I was wrong—Kenny's big *and* fast. With two giant steps, he gets in front of us again and blocks the sidewalk.

My stomach knots with dread when Kenny says, "Give it to me."

It doesn't sound like a demand, but I don't think Kenny's used to hearing the word *no*. I clutch the tin in my hand and try to think of a reason to refuse. "It's okay—I mean, no thanks. I mean . . ."

Kenny reaches out and snatches the tin from my hand. He shakes it, holding it close to his ear. "If there's nothing inside, why is it so hot?"

Vik pipes up. "That's part of the experiment."

"Right!" I cry. "It's—uh—trapped gas!"

Both Kenny and Vik look grossed out. I try to recover some of my cool. "But we're just going to buy a new tin of mints. I like mints. You do, too. Right, Vik?"

"Sure!" he replies with a wink. "Let's go to the store right now and get some more."

Kenny stares at us like we're the most pathetic people he's ever met. Then he surprises us again by saying, "I have this special spray at home. It helps you open lids that are stuck on jars." When Vik and I don't respond,

56

Kenny turns and starts walking away—with the tin in his hand!

"Come on," he says over his shoulder. "My house is this way."

I'm trying not to panic, but this is bad—really bad. I tug Vik's arm, but he just sighs and shrugs helplessly. Kenny's bigger than both of us. Even if we both jumped on him at the same time, we probably couldn't get the mint tin out of his hand. And we'd probably both end up getting clobbered.

Vik trails after Kenny, and I hurry to catch up. We cross the busy avenue and head down a quiet block lined with gray stone row houses. Kenny stops at one with a gas lamp flickering at the bottom of the stoop. He waves us up and unlocks the front door at the top of the stairs. Kenny drops his house key into one of the pockets on his vest and says, "My mom can be a bit . . . weird. Just ignore her—that's what I do."

Vik and I exchange nervous glances. Kenny seems to sense our unease, because he reaches past us to lock the vestibule door. "Don't worry," he says with a forced laugh. "We'll go out back—that's where my work-shop is."

We head down a long, dark hallway that ends in a

bright kitchen. Kenny's mother is perched on a stool, studying a cookbook.

"Hi, honey," she says absently, barely glancing up. "How was your walk?"

"Fine," Kenny says. Then he coughs so that his mother looks up from her book. When she sees me and Vik, her face lights up. She flings the book onto the counter and slides off the stool.

"You've brought friends home! How wonderful!" Mrs. O'Connor rushes over to shake our hands. "You're so welcome, boys. Call me Jo. Can I get you anything? Are you hungry?"

Kenny glares at us so we know what answer to give his mother.

"Can't talk now, Mom. We have a science project to work on."

"A science project—how exciting! Are you sure you wouldn't like a snack? I picked up some superfoods at the health food store so I could make those granola bites you like so much. You boys will need brain fuel to help you focus. Or how about a smoothie? I got some kale at the farmers' market yesterday. . . ."

"No time, Mom. We'll be out back." Kenny pushes past his mother, opens a sliding glass door at the back of the kitchen, and steps out onto a wooden deck.

Vik and I follow Kenny outside, stopping to say, "It was nice meeting you, Mrs. O'Connor."

"Just call me Jo," she says with a warm smile. "I'll fix a tray and bring it out in just a few minutes. Would that be all right, Kennedy?"

Kenny just gives his mother a dismissive backward wave as he disappears down the deck stairs. We follow him across a tidy lawn to a small wooden shed in the far corner of the yard. When we're all inside, he closes the door and slides a bolt lock into place.

"No one will bother us in here. Sorry about my mom. She's freaking out because she thinks I don't have any friends."

I don't blame her—at school Kenny is a loner. I figure he doesn't need me to remind him of that fact, but Vik blurts, "Well, do you?"

Kenny scowls and shrugs at the same time. Then softly he says, "Maybelline was my friend."

"Who's Maybelline?" Vik asks.

Kenny points to a photograph held by magnets to the door of a metal storage cabinet. "Maybelline's my nanny. Well, not anymore. My mom takes care of me now."

Vik and I exchange glances more carefully this time, but Kenny can't see us because his eyes are on the photo of Maybelline. She's an older Black woman with a warm smile and a gap between her two front teeth. To our surprise, Kenny continues in a mournful voice.

"Maybelline was the best. She was, like, my first real friend."

We don't know what to say, but when Kenny suddenly scans our faces for signs of mockery, we nod sympathetically.

"My papa had an ayah—that's what we call nannies in India," Vik says. "She still lives with us. Aunty's like a hundred years old!"

Kenny's eyes open wide. "Maybelline wasn't that old. She said that when it comes to friends, it's quality, not quantity, that matters most. A lot of kids at our school are jerks. I don't really care if they don't want to be friends with me."

Vik must be feeling brave, because he says, "They're probably just afraid of you, Kenny. You're kind of intimidating, you know."

"No, I'm not," Kenny says.

I wish there was a mirror in his workshop so Kenny could see himself the way we see him. "Actually, Kenny, you *are* a little scary. I mean, it's just because you're so . . . well . . ."

"I'm not fat!" Kenny cries, his freckled cheeks flushing red.

I jump back and stammer, "I—I know. Uh—I wasn't going to say—I mean, I was just trying to say . . ."

"What?" Kenny snarls.

Vik shifts his feet so he's standing closer to me. Kenny could pound us both with one blow, but it helps to know that Vik's got my back.

Vik clears his throat and says, "Face it, Kenny. You're massive."

Kenny glares at us, unsure whether to be offended by Vik's choice of words.

"'Massive' as in 'really strong,'" I add.

Vik nods. "Yeah—you're . . . powerful."

I'm not sure if Kenny believes us, but some of the anger goes out of his eyes. "I'm not a bully," he says sullenly. "It's those other kids who pick on me!"

I have *never* seen anybody picking on Kenny O'Connor. No one at our school is brave enough—or stupid enough—to do that.

"Why would anyone pick on you?" Vik asks.

Kenny shrugs and looks back at the photo of Maybelline on the cabinet. There's another photo, of a man with two boys. It looks like they're camping near a river.

The man's face has been scribbled over with a pen. He's wearing the same vest that Kenny's got on now.

"School is hard for me," Kenny says quietly. "Reading is, at least. The words get all mixed up."

"Maybe you're dyslexic," Vik says.

"So what if I am?" Kenny barks.

Vik holds up his hands like he's ready to surrender. "It's not such a big deal. My cousin has dyslexia, so reading is hard for him, but he just takes it slow. And he's really good at math. Somehow numbers don't move around as much as letters. For him, anyway."

Kenny sinks onto a folding chair and seems to relax. "For a while, I went to this school that had special services for kids like me."

"So how'd you end up at our school?" I ask.

"I got suspended."

"What'd you do?" Vik asks.

Kenny tries to stifle a smile. "I threw a desk at the wall."

"And you wonder why you don't have any friends!"

For a second or two, there's an awkward silence in the shed. Then all three of us burst out laughing. Kenny opens a drawer under the table and pulls out a rag. "Here—hold this," he says without looking at either of us.

I take the soft, clean rag from him and glance at Vik. Kenny's not so bad after all. But what will he do when the tin finally opens and a magical butterfly tumbles out?

Kenny pulls a key out of his pocket and unlocks a small gold padlock. He slides a chain that's wrapped around the handles of the metal cabinet, which takes up quite a bit of the shed. "This used to be my dad's," Kenny explains. "Now I keep all my stuff in here." He reaches up to the top shelf of the cabinet and takes down a spray bottle. "My mom bought this a while ago. When my dad left, she used to sit on the couch in her bathrobe watching TV all day. She'd watch a lot of infomercials and order just about everything. Most of the stuff was garbage, but this spray really works!"

"Listen, Kenny," Vik says suddenly. "We've got to come clean. This isn't part of a science project."

A smug grin spreads across Kenny's face. "I know," he says simply. "I just told my mom that so she'd leave us alone. I knew that you two were up to something as soon as I saw you sitting on that stoop."

Vik looks at me and nods as if to say, "Your turn." I take a deep breath. We have no choice but to tell Kenny everything.

"Do you believe in magic?" I ask tentatively.

Kenny looks at me, then at Vik, and then down at the

tin in his hand. He thinks for a moment before saying, "I guess."

Suddenly, there's a knock at the door. Vik and I jump as the doorknob rattles, but Kenny just raises his finger to his lips.

"Kennedy? I brought you and your friends some snacks. Are you in there? Of course you are—you must be hard at work. Well, I'll just leave this tray here outside the door, and you can get it whenever you're ready. Okay? I'm going back in the house now, but you can just text me if you need anything."

We hear Mrs. O'Connor set down the tray. Her footsteps make no sound as they cross the lawn, but we can hear her climbing the deck stairs. Only then does Kenny slide open the bolt on the door. He nods at Vik and says, "I'll open the door. You grab the tray."

Vik nods back and does as he's told, pausing to wave at Kenny's mother, who is still standing on the deck. Kenny closes the door and inspects the contents of the tray once Vik sets it on the table. There are three tumblers filled with thick green sludge, a bowl of mixed berries, and a plate covered in square cookies made with a whole lot of seeds.

"Not as bad as it could be," Kenny says. "But my mother's snacks always need a little improving."

Kenny opens the cabinet, and this time we see an entire shelf filled with junk food. He takes down a jar of chocolate hazelnut spread and a bottle of butterscotch syrup. "Help yourself," he says before dipping one of the seed cookies into the chocolate spread.

Vik does the same and nods appreciatively. "Not bad," he declares with a full mouth.

I pick up one of the tumblers and take a sip. "Ugh!"

"Yeah," Kenny says. "There's no real way to improve kale. Want a soda?"

I look at the bottled beverages Kenny has lined up inside his cabinet. "Water, please."

He hands me a bottle, and I thank him before taking a few swigs. Then I take a deep breath and bring us back to the matter at hand. "Here's the deal, Kenny. A few days ago, I went to another world—the realm of magic."

Kenny pauses to lick the chocolate off his lips. "How'd you get there?" he asks.

"I took a transporter, but I wasn't alone. I was making an important delivery. But when I got there, something was missing."

"Stolen by my bratty little sister," Vik says bitterly.

"So the . . . people I was working for sent me back to this world. And they sent something—someone—along to help me find what I lost."

65

Kenny nods as if all of this is making sense to him. Then he asks, "What'd you lose?"

I swallow hard and say, "A baby dragon."

Kenny doesn't even blink. He just gently taps his fingertip on the mint tin. "And what's in here?"

I swallow again and say, "A magic butterfly."

Kenny's unblinking gaze shifts from me to Vik and then back to me.

"For real?"

"For real. We're on a mission, but you don't have to get involved, Kenny. Just don't tell anyone about what's inside that tin—please."

"Who would I tell?" Kenny asks with half a grin. "I don't have any friends." He wipes his hands on his pants and gives the tin a few squirts before setting the bottle down. "Ready?" he asks us.

"Ready," Vik answers for us both.

Kenny uses the rag to get a grip on the oily tin. Through a combination of pulling and twisting, he manages to loosen the lid. We watch breathlessly as Kenny sets the tin down on the table and gives the lid one final tug.

With a loud popping sound, the lid comes off, and our mouths fall open in shock. There's no butterfly inside the tin—there's a tiny red person! It yawns and stretches its limbs before climbing out of the tin and onto the table.

"Is it . . . an elf?" Vik asks.

I can't reply, because I don't know the answer to that question. It was a butterfly—not an elf—that lit up the darkness of the transporter when Ma and I returned from the realm of magic. This creature is as new to me as it is to Vik and Kenny.

When the creature is certain it has our attention, it leans forward and makes a strange noise—like a long, loud sneeze. Something pops out of its back, and we watch in amazement as two shimmering wings slowly unfurl. The wings beat slowly two or three times before flapping so fast that the creature lifts into the air like a hummingbird.

"Whoa," Kenny whispers. The awe in his voice makes me think he just might keep his promise. "That's incredible—and so beautiful!"

The creature turns toward Kenny and lets its bright yellow eyes slowly sweep over him. Kenny blushes and looks away. The creature nods at him as if it approves before turning to Vik and me. I wonder if it will remember me, but the look of disdain on the creature's face assures me it hasn't forgotten what I've done.

"She's a fairy!" Vik cries.

"How do you know it's a girl?" I ask.

Vik rolls his eyes. "All fairies are girls." Then he thinks a moment and adds, "Aren't they?"

We take a closer look at the flying creature. All I can tell from watching the fairy is that it seems kind of vain.

Kenny makes no effort to hide his admiration. "Are you hungry?" he asks the fairy.

Without waiting for a response, Kenny takes a chocolate bar out of the cabinet. He snaps a square off and offers it to the fairy. It leans forward, sniffs it, and then takes a tiny bite. The creature's eyes close as it savors the sweet treat. But then it wanders over to the tray to examine the other options. The fairy picks up a blueberry and eats it the way we'd eat an apple. Then it flies up to the rim of my glass. To our surprise, the fairy bends down and uses its hand to ladle the kale smoothie into its mouth.

"Gross! I think she likes it," Vik said.

Kenny rummages through the table drawer until he finds a red cocktail straw. "Here—use this," he says to the fairy.

It would take forever for me to suck anything through such a narrow straw, but the fairy plunges the red straw into the smoothie and starts drinking. We all watch in silence as the tiny creature drains the tumbler of its slimy green fluid in less than a minute. After loudly sucking up the last of the smoothie, the fairy flits back to the tabletop and belches loudly.

Kenny laughs and says, "You're awesome!" Then he turns to me, his face glowing with excitement. "I can't believe you have a fairy—a real live fairy! What's its name?"

Vik turns to me as well, but all I can do is shrug. "I don't know. The *butterfly* belonged to Sis, not me."

"You don't have a sister," Vik reminds me before mumbling, "Lucky for you."

"It's like how it is with Ma," I explain. "She isn't anybody's mother, but that's what everyone calls her. Sis is . . ." I think back to that moment in the orange tent when Sis breathed fire into her palm. I knew as soon as we met that Sis didn't like me—even before she found out I'd lost one of her precious dragons. Just the memory of her scowl sends a shiver down my spine. "Sis is, like . . . a dragon lady."

The fairy doesn't seem to appreciate that comparison, because it scowls before hurling a blueberry at me.

I duck and say, "I like dragons! I'm just not very good at keeping track of them."

"So what should we call the fairy?" Kenny asks. Then he leans down and politely asks, "Do you have a name?"

The tiny red creature nods before flying over to the open cabinet. It points at a jar of grape jelly. Then it scans the shelves and finds a bottle of glass cleaner. It points to a third product before looking at us expectantly. When it's clear we don't understand, the fairy points to each of the product labels, over and over, in the same order until finally Vik cries, "It's spelling out its name! J-e-f."

"Jef? That can't be right," I say. "Can it?"

Kenny frowns. "What's wrong with Jef?"

"That's a boy's name," I say.

"No, it isn't!" Kenny barks. "And what if it is?" he asks in the same breath. "If the fairy says his name's Jef, that's what we're gonna call him!"

Kenny stops yelling when he realizes Vik and I are pressed up against the wall of the shed. We can't get farther away from him unless we open the door and run, and we can't leave the shed without the fairy. And the fairy—Jef—doesn't look like he's going anywhere without Kenny. Jef is perched on his left shoulder, smiling smugly like Kenny's his new best friend—and bodyguard.

"What do you need Jef to do?" Kenny asks once he's had a moment to calm down.

"I don't know what the fairy *can* do," I tell him. "I guess I hoped he could help me get in touch with my grandfather."

Kenny turns his head and asks Jef, "Can you do that?"

7

KAVITA

Aunty and I look around the streets of Jackson Heights. "We never had lunch," she says. "Are you hungry?"

I nod and look up the block. There are lots of restaurants to choose from. "Should we go to Manju Masi's place?"

Aunty clucks her tongue. "Then we'd have to eat her food. And I'm sure your mummy has called everyone in the family to tell them I kidnapped you. We'd better eat here instead."

Aunty puts her hand on my shoulder and steers me across the street and into a crowded shop with a red awning. We squeeze past the customers waiting at the counter to buy sweets. I follow her to the back of the shop, where there are tables for dining in. Most of them are empty, so we sit at a table for four next to the wall, even though there are just two of us. Well, three if you include Mo. I think the dragon can smell the sweets we passed, because when I lift the shawl, I find Mo anxiously pacing the cage. When the dragon starts to whine, I drop the shawl and ask Aunty if we should get Mo something to eat.

"On our way out. Best not to draw attention to your little friend, I think."

I nod and Aunty waves a waiter over to our table. "Dal makhani, kadai paneer, and two samosas, please. And two chai as well."

When the waiter brings over our chai in white cups and saucers, Aunty immediately reaches for the sugar dispenser. She holds the glass jar upside down, and a steady stream of cane sugar pours into her chai. Finally, I ask, "Can I have some sugar, Aunty?"

She looks up at me, surprised. Then Aunty smiles and hands the dispenser to me and starts stirring her chai.

I don't put quite as much sugar in my cup, but I like my chai sweet, too. I take a sip of the milky spiced tea and ask, "Do you think Bejan is right, Aunty?"

Aunty takes a sip of her sugary chai and sighs with her eyes closed. "Just right," she says before taking another sip. I wonder if Aunty has forgotten my question, but then she looks at me and says, "I've never known Bejan to misread the stars."

I sip my chai and try to decide whether to ask my next question. Aunty isn't looking at me, but she knows something's on my mind.

"Say what you have to say, child."

I set my cup on its saucer and wait for Aunty to look at me. "Why did Bejan say you were going on a journey?"

Aunty lowers her eyes and stirs her chai for a while. "We all have a purpose, child. I have spent a long time wondering what mine is. Now, thanks to your little friend, I think I know."

Before I can ask a follow-up question, the waiter arrives with our food. Aunty hands me the plate with my samosa, and suddenly I forget all about "purpose" and journeys and dig into our delicious meal.

When we finish eating, Aunty pays the bill and leads me over to the counter, where the sweets are kept. Even though my belly is full, my mouth starts to water as I gaze at all the creamy treats behind the glass. Mo must sense that sweets are nearby, because the dragon starts scampering around in the cage. I hurry outside, leaving Aunty behind to make her purchase. She joins us a moment later, a small red box poking out of her purse.

"What do we do now?" I ask.

"Now we find a taxi," Aunty replies.

It's always loud in the city, so when we hear a blaring car horn, we don't think anything of it. But then I hear someone calling my name and see Manju Masi on the other side of the intersection. She isn't honking at us—it's the car behind her. Manju Masi is blocking traffic by standing outside her car, frantically waving at us. She has her phone pressed to her ear. I can't hear her, but I know what she's telling Mummy: *I've found them.*

Aunty grabs hold of my shoulder and steers me toward the entrance to the subway. "Quick—down here!" she cries.

There are so many people coming up the stairs that going down—with a birdcage in my arms—is pretty challenging. But Aunty has a firm grip on my shoulder, and she uses me as a sort of shield. Some people show respect for her age and veer out of the way.

I can still hear Manju Masi calling our names on the street up above. Aunty rushes us over to the agent in the booth and buys a single-ride MetroCard. I hand the cage to Aunty, scramble under the turnstile, and then take back the cage so Aunty can swipe her card and pass through as well. We weave our way through the press of people coming and going, and finally squeeze onto a train just as the familiar ding-dong sound signals the closing of the doors.

"Good heavens," Aunty says, fanning herself with Bejan's flyer. A young man with giant headphones clamped over his ears gets up and offers Aunty his seat. She thanks him and sinks onto the bench. I rest the cage on Aunty's knees and look up at the map on the wall of the train.

"We'll have to switch trains to get back to Brooklyn," I tell Aunty.

"A taxi would have been easier," Aunty says, "but we must do the best we can with what we have."

Another passenger gets up, and I squeeze onto the bench next to Aunty. "I like taking the train," I tell her.

"I think your little friend finds the subway a bit cramped," Aunty replies.

I look around the car we're on. It isn't rush hour yet, so the train isn't packed. Then I lift the shawl to check on Mo and gasp before dropping the cloth again. Mo is growing! No wonder the cage felt so much heavier. We haven't given Mo any peda yet. It must be the mint Mo found under Bejan's desk.

"What do we do?" I ask, unable to hide the alarm I feel.

Aunty looks at her watch. "It will take us close to an hour to reach Brooklyn by train."

Mo whines pitifully as its body presses against the bars of the cage. Aunty and I move to the far end of the car, where there are fewer people. Aunty sings a lullaby that seems to soothe the unhappy dragon. When it's time to switch trains, Aunty and I wait on the platform until all the other passengers head toward the exit. Then Aunty lifts the shawl while I open the door and try to squeeze Mo out of the cage. I have to bend the metal bars, but eventually the dragon squeezes out. Aunty quickly drapes the shawl over Mo, and I scoop the growing dragon up in my arms.

When Mo licks my face, I smell mint on the dragon's breath. "Oh, Mo!" I sigh. Caring for a baby dragon is more difficult than I thought it would be.

"Keep its head covered," Aunty advises. "Hopefully, people will think it's just a toy."

We head for the train that will take us back to Brooklyn. When we finally arrive, Aunty and I climb the stairs and exit the station. I wanted to take the elevator, but Aunty said we needed to avoid getting close to other people.

"Where are we going?" I ask, breathing heavily. Our

home is just a few blocks away, but Aunty's walking in the opposite direction.

"Bejan said the gate was housed in a tall structure," Aunty reminds me.

"A tower," I say softly, thinking of the many churches in our neighborhood. One has a bell tower. I hear the bells chiming every hour. Could the gate to the realm of magic be in a church?

"This way," Aunty says.

While we're standing at the corner waiting for the light to change, I see a stroller abandoned next to the overflowing trash can. Suddenly, I have an idea. I ask Aunty to hold Mo for a moment. Then I brush the crumbs and candy wrappers off the seat and test out the stroller's wheels. One of the front wheels wobbles so badly that it's hard to make the stroller move in a straight line. I guess that's why it's been thrown away.

I sigh and hold my arms out so Aunty can give the dragon back to me. "It's not perfect," I tell Mo, "but it will have to do. You're too heavy for me to carry."

When we get across the street, a man comes up to us. He's wearing a baseball cap and mirrored sunglasses and has the collar of his denim jacket turned up. Without saying a word to me or Aunty, he squats in front of the stroller and grins at Mo.

"What a beautiful baby," the man says.

Then he tilts his head up at me, and my mouth falls open. Every inch of the man's face is covered in tattoos. And they're moving!

"You shouldn't walk around with something so precious," he tells me. "Anything could happen."

Aunty tightens her grip on my shoulder. "We can manage, thank you. Now, if you don't mind, we have a rather urgent appointment. . . ."

"Indeed, you do! Which is why you should have an escort," the man insists. "Allow me," he says, taking over the handles of the stroller. "The gate you're looking for is this way."

Aunty doesn't say a word, but I gasp. How could this strange man know about that?

He looks back over his shoulder and smiles at us. "Coming?"

Aunty grabs hold of my hand and gives it a squeeze. Then we follow the tattooed man up Franklin Avenue.

8

JAXON

Jef smiles at Kenny and flies over to the table. He kicks at the tray until Vik moves it out of the way. Once he has enough room, Jef hovers a few inches above the table and closes his eyes. Jef holds up his arms like a ballet dancer and then lowers them slowly as his wings beat faster.

"What's he doing?" Vik asks me.

"I don't know," I whisper, "but it looks like Jef's concentrating really hard."

"SHHH!" Kenny hisses at us.

Jef raises his arms once more, but this time when he lowers them, a circle of blue light appears. It's as if the fairy traced a bubble in the air and then willed it into existence. I don't have time to be astonished, because suddenly I hear a man's voice.

"Is this thing working? Can you hear me?"

I peer into the blue bubble and see L. Roy's face looking back at me. His head is huge and his body is small,
the way people look through the peephole in our front
door.

"L. Roy!" I cry with relief. "Is my granddad there? I
need his help."

"Jaxon? Have you found the dragon?" L. Roy looks
over his shoulder and nervously adds, "Please tell me
you got it back."

"Uh . . . not yet. But we know where it is . . . pretty much. Listen, L. Roy, I need your help. Ma's sick. She went to bed as soon as we got back from the realm of magic, and she hasn't gotten up since. It's like all her energy's gone."

L. Roy shakes his head. "I was afraid that might happen. The dragons you left here aren't doing well, either. Sis is tending to them now. She's awfully angry, Jax. If you can't get that dragon back here soon, Sis will come get it herself. And you *definitely* don't want that."

He's right—I don't. But I have to make him understand what I'm up against. "Ambrose is gone, and the transporters aren't working. Once I find the dragon, how do I get it back to the realm of magic?"

"I wish I could help you, son, but we're having the same problem over here. In fact, your granddad's out there now, searching for a way to get back to you."

"Why is this happening?" I ask helplessly, fighting to hold back tears. Vik gives my shoulder a squeeze, and that reminds me to take a deep breath.

L. Roy sighs heavily and takes off his spectacles. He rubs his eyes. "I blame myself for this mess. I was so sure those dragons would fix the imbalance that's been building over the years. But I was wrong," L. Roy confesses. "It's too late. And now you and Ma are mixed up in my mistake."

I take another deep breath. "We can still make things right. Just tell me what to do, L. Roy."

L. Roy shakes his head as he puts his glasses back on. "You're just a kid. Ma never even had a chance to begin your training."

Hearing the defeat in L. Roy's voice makes me realize I'm not ready to give up. "There's got to be something I can do," I insist. "There are all those books in Ma's apartment—tell me which one to read."

"What you need isn't in any book, Jax. There's only one person who can get you back to the realm of magic."

"Trub?" I ask hopefully.

L. Roy shakes his head and clears his throat. He glances over his shoulder once more before leaning in close. His head swells like a balloon, and I fight the urge to laugh.

"There's a . . . gatekeeper. He was, er, demoted a few years back, but . . . he might know of a gap between the two worlds."

"That's great!" I cry. "Where can I find this gate-keeper?"

To my surprise, L. Roy laughs. "Blue has a sweet tooth. If he's got any teeth left, he'll be sinking them into something sugary."

I wait for L. Roy to go on, but after a few seconds, it's

clear he's said all he has to say. "That's it? That doesn't really tell me where to find this . . . Blue person."

"Sorry, Jax. Blue's been off my radar for some time now. He's . . . unreliable. And unpredictable. Last time I saw Blue, he was scarfing down doughnuts."

I jump when Kenny suddenly joins the conversation. I'd forgotten that he and Vik are in the shed, too.

"That doesn't help," Kenny complains. "There are hundreds of doughnut shops in New York."

Vik adds, "And tons of food trucks sell doughnuts, too."

L. Roy frowns. "Who's that? Jax—you're not alone?"

"I'm with my friends. They're here to help me," I assure him.

"Magic is serious business, Jax. You can't tell ordinary people what's going on—they won't understand. And wasn't it your 'friend' who stole the dragon?"

"That was my sister—not me!" Vik blurts out.

"It's okay, L. Roy. I trust them. And until you and Trub get here, I need a crew of my own."

L. Roy thinks for a moment before giving me a grudging nod. "Well, be careful. If you do find Blue, he'll know you're desperate. He'll want to strike a bargain, but just remember that he's—"

Just then, the fairy drops to the table and collapses

in a tiny heap. The blue bubble disappears—and so does L. Roy.

"You wore Jef out," Kenny says, gently scooping the exhausted creature up in his hand.

"Should we put him back in the tin?" Vik asks.

I nod, but Kenny glares at us. "Would *you* want to be crammed into that tiny tin?"

"No," I admit, "but we can't walk around Brooklyn with a fairy!"

Kenny looks at his vest and says, "Jef can ride with me." He carefully deposits the fairy in one of his pockets and then puts his hands on his hips. "So, how do we find Blue?"

I glance at Vik, who looks just as surprised as me. "Uh, you don't have to come with us, Kenny."

Kenny's mouth falls open, and his cheeks turn pink. He looks surprised and disappointed. "But . . . I helped you open the tin. And you told that L. Roy guy we were part of your crew."

"He *is* good with Jef," Vik reminds me.

Kenny nods in agreement. "I can help in other ways, too. I know my way around the neighborhood. And— well, like you said before, I'm massive!"

I think about that for a moment. Having a friend Kenny's size might come in handy. But if anything happened to him, it'd be my fault. "I don't know, Kenny. What if—"

Kenny doesn't give me a chance to finish. "There's a doughnut shop on Empire Boulevard, near the park. We should start there."

"There's one on Bedford Avenue, too. We could check both places," Vik suggests.

"I have a better idea," I say. "But I'm going to need your help, and, well, things might get a little messy."

Kenny shrugs. "That doesn't bother me. I like getting my hands dirty."

"I'm going to remind you of that later," I warn him. Then I slide the bolt and open the shed door. "Let's get going. We have a rat to find!"

9

JAXON

"Did he say 'rat'?" Kenny asks.

"Ugh! Rats are disgusting," Vik says.

"You'll like Nate," I assure them. "He's really clever, and he can sniff out just about anything or anyone. He knew your sister had taken the dragon."

"How could he know that?" Vik asks. "Is he psychic?"

I shake my head and grin. "Nate told us he could smell a thief. I didn't realize it at the time, but he was talking about Kavita."

Kenny nods as my plan becomes clear. "So you think this rat can sniff out Blue?"

"Nate's our best bet," I reply confidently. "We just have to find him."

Kenny locks up the shed and leads us back across the lawn and into his house. He says, "Bye, Mom! We gotta go to the library so we can finish up our project. I've got my phone. I'll text you when we get there."

Before Kenny's mom can object, we dash out of the house and into the street. I head up the block even though I'm not sure just where I'm leading my friends.

"How are we going to find this clever rat?" Vik asks, hurrying to keep up.

"Just look for a mound of smelly garbage," Kenny says.

All the bins by the curb are empty, which means the sanitation trucks have already collected the household garbage.

"We could check the subway," Vik says. "I always see rats scurrying along the tracks when I'm waiting for the train."

These are good suggestions, but the last time I saw Nate, he took a different route to get underground. "I think Nate lives in the sewer."

"I am *not* crawling into a sewer!" Kenny declares.

We all know he couldn't fit even if he were willing. But I've seen kids reach deep into a drain when their ball has rolled into the opening at the curb. It's dangerous, but they still do it. If Mama knew I was thinking about crawling into a sewer, she'd be so disappointed in me. And she'd blame Ma. I definitely don't want that.

"Maybe Jef could go down and take a look," I say.

Kenny looks horrified by the idea. He gently pats his pocket and says, "Jef needs to rest a bit longer. Why don't we check the dumpsters behind that supermarket over there?"

That's a reasonable idea, so we cross the street and peer down the alley. Three dumpsters are overflowing with bags of trash. A black cat lurks around the entrance to the alley but doesn't seem willing to navigate the murky puddles and rancid air.

"After you," Vik says.

I try holding my breath but eventually give up and surrender to the stinking alley. There are sounds of life all around us, but I don't see any rats.

Suddenly, Kenny yells, "Over there!"

I follow his pointing finger and see two rats fighting over a half-eaten slice of pizza.

"Is that him?" Vik asks.

I study the two rats for a moment and shake my head. "I don't think so. Nate's bigger than that, and . . . well, more dignified."

"Maybe you should ask those rats if they know where Nate is," Vik suggests.

I feel a little ridiculous speaking to a couple of rats, but just this morning I was talking to a squirrel and a pigeon, so I give it a try.

"Excuse me, we're looking for a friend of ours. His name is Nate. Have you seen him?"

The rats abandon their tug-of-war for a moment. While one rodent rises up on its haunches and sniffs the air, seeming to consider my question, the other one scurries away with the disgusting slice. The rat that lost out shakes its fist at me but doesn't answer my question. Suddenly, I hear a familiar voice behind us.

"You lookin' for me?"

We spin around and find Nate leaning up against the metal dumpster with his arms folded across his chest.

"Nate! Am I glad to see you. We need your help."

"So I heard. What's up, kid?"

"We're looking for a guy named Blue. Can you tell us where to find him?"

Nate shudders. "Blue's a nasty piece of work. Trash, really—and I know a thing or two about trash!" Nate chuckles and then grows serious once more. "You want to stay as far away from Blue as possible, kid."

"Why? L. Roy gave us his name. He said Blue's a gatekeeper."

"*Former* gatekeeper. Blue can't be trusted. He'll only help you if there's something in it for him. He hasn't got a selfless bone in his freaky blue body."

"He's actually blue?" Kenny asks, amazed.

"Blue can be holy. Lord Krishna is blue. Lord Shiva, too," Vik says.

"This Blue definitely isn't divine. He gets his name from his unusual tattoos. They give his skin a strange hue—and make my skin crawl! That dude is bad news," Nate says, shaking his head.

"But the transporters aren't working and Ambrose is gone. We have to find another way to reach the realm of magic."

Nate sniffs at a moldy bread crust. "Blue won't help you out of the goodness of his heart. He'll expect to be paid."

Kenny fishes in the pockets of his vest and pulls out a bunch of crumpled bills. "How much?"

Nate snorts and hops up on a plastic milk crate with a half-eaten apple. He takes a bite and says, "You don't get it, kid. Money means nothing to a guy like Blue."

"What does he want?" I ask.

"Magic!" Nate cries.

Kenny's hand instinctively moves to the pocket where Jef is. "We haven't got any magic," he says.

Nate rolls his eyes and then sniffs the air. "You've got a fairy in your pocket, kid." Then he points at me. "And you've got a baby dragon born on *this* side of the divide."

"Er, not exactly. The dragon is with Vik's sister," I explain.

"I know." Nate turns to Vik and says, "Your sister's close by."

"No, she's not. Kavita's with my aunty out in Queens," Vik says.

Nate taps his snout. "I never forget a scent. The thief—and her dragon—are near!"

"Then we have to act fast!" I exclaim. "Just tell us where to find Blue. Once he tells us where the portal is, we'll make sure Kavita hands over the dragon. Please, Nate—we can do this!"

"You don't understand. Blue already knows why you need his help. He knows about the box L. Roy sent from Madagascar, and he knows that Trub took you to meet Sis and Ma in the realm of magic. He knows why you came back. He knows that Ma's health is failing—and that you'd do anything to make her better. Blue is a dangerous man! He crossed Sis once, but even she couldn't strip him of all his power. Listen, kid, your grandfather's been a good friend to me—he'd want me to look out for you. Forget about Blue. Give Trub some time to find a safe way to move between the two realms."

"We haven't got time!" I cry. "I think Ma's getting worse. And the dragons I did deliver—they're suffering, too. They need to be reunited with their sibling. I've got to make things right."

"You can't, kid. Things have been set in motion.

What's done can't be undone. The best plan is for you and your friends to go home. When Trub gets here, he'll collect the dragon and take it back to Sis."

"What if he can't find a way to get back to Brooklyn?" I ask.

"Your grandfather always comes through. Trust him, kid—I do."

Before any of us can say another word, Nate darts out of the alley, crosses the street, and disappears inside the sewer.

Kenny still has his hand protectively covering his pocket. "So—what's the plan?" he asks.

I'm not sure what to do. I was positive Nate would help us. I look to Vik and feel relieved when he offers a sensible solution.

"Let's start with the doughnut shop on Empire."

We check both doughnut shops in our neighborhood, but no one there fits the description. Kenny uses some of his crumpled-up bills to buy us each a doughnut. We thank him and head up to the park.

"Well, that was a waste of time," Kenny says, licking at the sprinkles stuck to his fingers.

"Not necessarily," Vik says. "Nate swears my sister's close by—we didn't know that before."

"Why don't you call her and find out just where she's at?" I suggest.

Vik tries calling his aunt's phone, but neither she nor Kavita picks up. He leaves a message telling them to meet us in the park across the street from the old spice factory.

I look around the park and marvel at how ordinary everything looks. Kids are laughing and playing tag around the jungle gym. Older boys race up and down the basketball court, their ball thudding loudly as they dribble on the asphalt. A couple of older men are even using the handball court. They don't know anything about our "mission." A small part of me wishes I could be ordinary, too.

"It always smells funny around here," Kenny says.

It does. I nod at the building across the street from the park. "It's the spices they make over there, I guess."

"The sign says they're an importer of spices," Vik points out. "I don't think they make anything in that old building."

"Then why is there a smokestack?" I ask.

"I think it used to be a different kind of factory. Look up there." Vik points to a smooth patch on the brick wall that's been framed by blocks of stone of a different color. "Someone has removed an inscription. That must have been the name of the original factory."

Kenny crinkles up his forehead and studies the smooth patch of stone for a long while. He opens his mouth to say something, then looks at the ground instead.

"Whatever that place used to be, it just looks creepy now," I say.

Graffiti covers the dark brown brick walls, and all the ground-level doors are sealed off. The ground-floor windows are caged and barred, and the loading dock doesn't seem to be in use. There's just one wide entrance for vehicles that leads to a cobblestone courtyard. Next to

the building is an empty lot. A tall chain-link fence surrounds the lot, and dingy plastic bags flutter listlessly in the breeze, snared by the razor wire that loops along the top of the fence.

Suddenly, I hear a shrill whistle. Thinking it might be Soot, the pigeon I met this morning, I start examining the birds strutting around the park. Then the whistle pierces the air again and I realize it's coming from behind us. I look over my shoulder and find a glowing blue man staring at me.

I nudge Vik and Kenny. "I think we've found Blue—or he's found us."

10

JAXON

The table Blue's seated at is set up for a game of chess, but I don't see an opponent. Kenny and Vik follow me as I go over to talk to Blue.

"Have a seat, kid," he says in a friendly voice. Then he produces a box of doughnuts and holds it out to me. "Want one?"

"No, thanks," I tell him as I slide onto the stone bench. Kenny and Vik stand behind me. I can't tell if they're trembling like I am. I swallow hard and say, "You must be Blue."

He laughs and looks at his bare arms. "I guess I am. It's the ink. I'm not blue, really."

I can't even count all the tattoos on Blue's body. Every inch of his bare arms is covered by serpents, and mermaids, and plenty of other symbols and words I've never seen before. The freaky thing is, Blue's tattoos are *alive*.

The serpent winds its way up and down his left arm before circling his neck and slithering down his right arm. The mermaid winks and waves at me as she bobs on the waves, and a panther seems to prowl across Blue's bald head as it stalks a hummingbird. He even has tattoos on his face! A silver nose ring hangs above his thin lips, which are also a deep shade of blue.

"Did it hurt?" Kenny asks. "Getting all those tattoos?"

"Not a bit," Blue says before sinking his teeth into a jelly doughnut. When he uses his tongue to catch a glob of red jelly that squirts out, we see that even his tongue is covered in tattoos!

"These are my guests," Blue explains. "Roommates, if you will. We share space and show respect. Everyone gets along because I'm a good host." Blue's gaze flicks to Kenny—or his pocket, to be more precise. Then his pale gray eyes return to me. "Real ink tattoos are permanent, but these . . . these are just temporary."

"You mean you can . . . remove them?"

"Absolutely!" Blue confirms. "And that's what I intend to do—when the time is right. For now I'm just something of a collector. A conservationist, if you will."

After everything Nate told us, I didn't expect Blue to be so laid-back. "Do you play chess?" I ask.

He grins. "When I find a worthy opponent. Want to play?"

My dad taught me how to play chess, but it would be hard to concentrate with Blue's tattoos roaming all over his body. "Maybe another time," I say. "Right now we need your help."

Blue sets the box of doughnuts at the edge of the table and leans in closer to me. "Sounds serious. What do you need, kid?"

I glance over my shoulder at Vik and Kenny. It helps knowing they've got my back, but I wish I could let someone else do the talking right now. They didn't make this mess, though—I did. It's up to me to clean it up.

"I need a portal—or a working transporter. L. Roy— that's a friend of mine—he said you might know of a 'gap' that could get me . . . where I need to go."

Blue nods to show that he's taking me seriously. Then he leans back and rubs his chin, which sends a couple of hornets buzzing up to his forehead.

"The professor sent you to me, did he?"

I nod, relieved that Blue knows L. Roy. Hopefully, that will make him trust me.

Blue links his fingers and looks straight into my eyes. "What are you offering?" he asks simply.

It's not a demand, but I still feel a knot twisting in my stomach. "Wh-what do you mean?"

"I'm sure the professor told you that I don't work for free, kid. I operate on the barter system. I give you something you want, and you give me something I want. That's fair, right?"

Everything Blue's saying makes sense. I glance back at Vik, who says, "Tell us what you want."

Blue grins, and once again I feel uneasy. There's something oily about his smile. He licks the white powdered sugar off his lips and leans in once more. "Tell me what you've got," he says quietly.

If Nate's right about Blue, this is just a game. He already knows about the dragon. So why waste time?

"We have a fairy," I tell him, knowing Kenny might clobber me right then and there.

A smirk twists Blue's mouth. "Have you, now? Can I see it?"

I have no choice now but to turn and face Kenny. His cheeks have turned red, but he opens his pocket and Jef flies out. The fairy sweeps his eyes over Blue, folds his arms, and turns his back to Blue while hovering above the chessboard.

Blue laughs off the snub. "My, my, my," he says with

exaggerated admiration. "That's no ordinary fairy, boys. You've got one of Sis's personal attendants."

Jef refuses to turn around, but the haughty creature tilts his head up a bit. He's clearly proud that Blue knows who he is.

"That kind of fairy is highly prized in some circles," Blue says.

"What are you going to do with Jef?" Kenny demands.

"Do? What do you think I would do to such a gem? Your little friend will be right at home amongst my menagerie. I have several fairies already, but—it's Jef, is it? This one outranks them all."

"Wait—you mean . . . you mean you're going to turn

Jef into a tattoo?" Kenny reaches out a desperate hand, and Jef flies over to him. Kenny pulls the fairy close for protection and drops Jef into his pocket.

"It's just a temporary state of being," Blue assures us. "Until I can . . ."

"Until you can what?"

Blue looks sideways at Vik. "That's none of your concern." Then his gaze slides back to me. With a bright smile, he says, "A deal's a deal. The gate you're looking for is right behind you. Once you hand Jef over, I'll open it for you."

We all turn around, but there's nothing to see. "The gate's in this park?" I ask.

"Across the street," Blue says. "Inside that old factory." He glances at his wrist, but there's no watch there—just a strange tattoo of a compass with a needle that moves. "Meet me there in an hour and I can open the gate for you."

I study Blue for a moment. "How do we know you can deliver what you're promising? L. Roy said you were . . . demoted."

Blue's mouth twists as if he's just tasted something bitter. "L. Roy told you about that, did he? I suppose he would—he's guilty of the exact same crime. I'm just the one who got caught."

It's hard to believe L. Roy would ever commit a crime. Blue sees the doubt in my eyes and laughs at me.

"I guess the professor doesn't look like a criminal—but I do, right?"

"N-no," I stammer unconvincingly.

"L. Roy and I want the same thing. We used to, anyway."

"And what's that?" Vik asks warily.

"A new world," Blue says simply. "The old world, really. The professor and I want things to be the way they used to be, when magic was integrated into this world. One realm—not two."

"L. Roy says it's too late—the balance can't be restored."

"He's a quitter," Blue says with a sudden snarl. Then he grows calm and adds proudly, "I'm not. Every creature has the right to be free. I'm a liberator."

"I doubt Sis sees you that way," I counter.

Blue's lip curls slightly. "Sis. What do you know about her?"

"She's a guardian."

Blue shrugs. "You say guardian; I say jailer. She's holding these magical beasts against their will. Does that sound righteous to you? I, on the other hand, provide safe passage from one realm to the other. For those who are willing."

I think for a moment. "You're a smuggler, aren't you?"

Blue laughs. "There may be a pirate or two in my family tree, but I prefer to think of myself as an importer of rare and exotic creatures. I do what I have to do. Borders should be open. People, ideas, magic—all of it should flow freely."

"Sis found out, didn't she? That's why you were fired."

Blue makes a sound of contempt. "I was demoted—because somebody snitched. My money's on the professor. Or his gangly friend—what's his name? Prob, Problem. Something absurd."

I swallow hard. "Trouble?"

"Trub! That's the one. Amateur. Thinks he's a do-gooder, but they just use him to do jobs no one else wants to do."

Vik looks at me expectantly. I know I should defend my granddad, but something tells me to keep my mouth shut. We've told Blue too much already.

For a moment, Blue's eyes lock on mine, and I feel a shiver run up my spine. Kenny clutches his pocket protectively, as if Jef might be in danger. For the first time today, I'm glad the dragon is with Kavita and not me. I don't trust Blue, but he seems like our only option. If Nate's right and the dragon is close by, then all we have to do is find Kavita and get Blue to open the gate. That would mean giving up Jef, but something tells me that particular fairy can take care of himself.

I look at the chess pieces arranged before me. Dad always told me that chess was a game of strategy. You had to anticipate what your opponent might do. I decide to try stalling. "We need a little time to think about your offer."

Blue just shrugs. "The clock's ticking, kid. I ain't got all day—and neither do you."

I get up from the bench. "Well, we'll get out of your hair—er, I mean, we'll be on our way."

Blue studies me for a moment. "I don't think you understand. The gate will only open for a few minutes today—and I'm the only one who can open it."

I nod. "I get it. I just need to talk things over with my friends. We know where to find you."

"Suit yourself," Blue says as if it doesn't matter to him. "Here." He holds out the box of doughnuts. "Take some for the road."

None of us wants his leftover doughnuts, but I take

the box just so we can get out of there. I mumble a quick "thanks," and we hurry out of the park.

When we reach the corner, I drop the box of doughnuts into the trash.

"What a creep!" Kenny says, peering into his pocket to check on Jef. "You can't make a deal with him."

"I may not have a choice," I say.

Vik stares at the graffiti-covered building across the street. "Do we really need to make a deal with Blue? I mean, he just told us where the gate is. Think you can open it on your own, Jax?"

We cross the street and stand in front of the spice factory. It's hard to imagine a gate to the realm of magic inside this run-down building.

"I don't even know how we can get inside," I confess.

"That driveway must be for deliveries," Kenny says. "Let's go in that way."

Vik shakes his head. "We can't just walk in there. The people who work in the factory will want to know what we're up to."

"There's probably a back entrance. Maybe we could sneak in that way," I suggest.

We walk down the block to the empty lot at the corner. Vik examines the heavy chain and padlock wrapped around the fence gates. If Trub were here, he could easily pick that lock. But we're on our own. When Kenny pulls against the fence, the gates pull apart just enough for me and Vik to squeeze through. What we'll do once we're inside the lot, I don't know. But we have to take it one step at a time.

Kenny peeks inside his pocket and says, "I hope you're feeling stronger, Jef, because we could really use your help."

Jef's red head pokes out of the pocket and nods up at Kenny. Then the fairy rises into the air and leads us down the block. Jef points at the spot high on the factory wall where the previous company's name was erased.

Kenny frowns. "There it is again!" he says with a mixture of excitement and exasperation.

Vik and I follow his gaze. "What are you talking about, Kenny?"

"Don't you see it?" Kenny asks. "All that gold writing . . ."

Vik wipes his eyes, squints at the wall, and then looks at me. "Do you see anything?" he whispers.

I shake my head. "Read it out to us, Kenny."

It's only after I've made my request that I remember Kenny's dyslexic. His cheeks turn pink, and he jams his hands into the pockets of his vest. Jef perches on his shoulder and nods encouragingly. Kenny shifts from one foot to the other before clearing his throat. In a shaky voice he reads, "Esmeralda's Excellent Emporium: Exotic Spices, Magical Potions, and Mythical Creatures of All Kinds."

As soon as the last word leaves Kenny's lips, I feel something shift. The sun should set soon, but the air grows a bit warmer and the street suddenly becomes eerily quiet. The happy shrieks of playing kids and the steady thud of basketballs fade to silence. I look back across the street and find a field of tall pink grass swaying where the playground ought to be. The spice factory's facade has been scrubbed clean, and all the windows glisten with clear glass panes—no bars and no cages.

"Uh . . . g-guys?" I stammer. "I don't think we're in Brooklyn anymore."

11

JAXON

"What do you mean?" Vik asks. "We haven't moved—we're still standing in front of the old spice factory."

"I know, but look around," I urge. "Where's the basketball court? There's no graffiti on the walls. And check out the trees—they've got leaves!"

Vik looks up. "Golden leaves," he observes. "The leaves only turn that color in the fall."

Kenny's eyes grow wide. "Have we gone back in time?"

"I don't think so," I tell him. "But I think the words you read—the words only you could see, Kenny—triggered some kind of change."

"Well, if we're not in Brooklyn . . . where are we?"

I think for a moment. "Trub—my granddad—told me that the realm of magic sometimes mimics features of the real world."

"So . . . none of this is real?"

I reach down and crunch one of the dry yellow leaves between my fingers. "It's real. It just isn't our world. I think we're in the realm of magic—or close."

Vik looks at me skeptically. "But—how did we get here? You said the transporters weren't working."

"I know. But L. Roy said there could still be 'gaps,' and Blue said this is where the gate is. We must be in some type of in-between place."

Kenny points at the brick smokestack. "Look!" he cries.

We follow his finger and see orange smoke curling out of the top. The entrance at the bottom of the smokestack is no longer sealed with cement blocks. Instead, an elaborately carved wooden door stands slightly ajar. The sky above us is a beautiful shade of mauve, and a flock of silver birds dips and dives like a school of fish in the air. There are no towering baobabs here like the last time I visited the realm of magic, but I feel just as calm. I try to reassure my friends, since they look anything but calm right now.

"It's okay, you guys. We're safe here." When they look at me doubtfully, I rush on. "Really—this might even be a good thing. I really think we're close to the realm of magic. All we need now is the dragon!"

I turn to Vik, excitement bubbling inside me as a plan starts to form in my mind. "Quick—call your sister. If Blue's telling the truth, we don't have much time. She has to bring the dragon here right away!"

Vik takes out his phone, but as soon as he dials the number, we can tell something's wrong. "Aunty?" he says doubtfully before offering an apology. "Sorry—I must have dialed the wrong number."

"What happened?" I ask.

"A man answered," Vik tells us with a confused look

on his face. "Maybe my phone won't work in this . . . realm."

I hadn't thought of that. "Try again," I urge him.

Vik dials the number once more, but a queasy look soon appears on his face. "Aunty? Kavita? Who is this?" Vik demands. His hands start trembling, and he nearly drops the phone.

Kenny and I hear a man laughing loudly on the other end. The doughnut I ate earlier suddenly feels like a rock in my belly. "Hang up, Vik," I urge him. "Just hang up."

Instead, Vik grips his phone with both hands and yells, "What have you done to them? Why are you doing this?"

I grab the phone from Vik and end the call. Kenny looks from me to Vik and back to me. "What's going on?" he asks anxiously.

"Blue's got them," I say quietly.

Kenny swallows hard and manages to erase most of the fear that was in his eyes a moment ago. "Okay," he says. "So we have to open the gate *after* we rescue your sister and your aunt." Kenny plants his hands on his hips and asks me, "What's the plan?"

I think about what Ma said before we left the realm of magic together: "Sometimes you don't have time to make a plan. Sometimes you just have to use whatever you've got to do whatever you can."

I've got my friends. We've also got a fairy. Will that be enough?

Tears are shining in Vik's eyes. I put my arm around him and give my friend a reassuring squeeze. "Don't worry, Vik. Kavita and your aunt aren't far away. Blue's probably holding them inside the spice factory."

"So . . . does that mean he already has the dragon?" Kenny asks. "Why didn't he just say so?"

"I don't know," I confess. "It's like he's playing some kind of game. Nate did say we couldn't trust Blue."

"This is a trap," Vik says hopelessly. "Blue has everything, which means we have nothing to bargain with."

"That's not true," I say with more confidence than I actually feel.

Kenny sighs. "I guess you'll have to trade Vik's family for Jef."

The fairy seems untroubled by that possibility, but Kenny's clearly upset. I think for a moment. The first time we used the transporter, Ma had to give Ambrose a password. Trub didn't need a password because he picked the lock on the guardhouse. But there was one other time . . .

"Maybe not!" I insist. "There might be another way."

I slip my book bag off my shoulder and dig inside until I find the jagged fragment of crystal I collected when Ma and I went back in time—way back—all the way to the Jurassic era.

"What's that?" Kenny asks.

I open my palm, and the crystal sparkles even though I can't see a sun up in the sky. "It's quartz," I tell him. "Ma used a larger crystal to send me back to Brooklyn. Maybe we can use this rock to send the dragon back to the realm of magic." I don't tell them that Ma used a compression spell—a spell I don't know. I figure we'll cross that bridge when we get to it.

Suddenly, we hear a voice calling for help. It seems to be coming from the top floor of the factory.

Vik freezes. "That's my sister!"

We all look up, but it's Kenny who spots the one window that's open. "I think she's up there!" he cries.

Vik rushes over and calls up. "Kavita? Kavita—is that you?"

Kavita doesn't come to the window, but we can hear her clearly. "Vikram—help us! The scary man took Mo!"

"Who's Mo?" Kenny asks us.

Before we can answer, the window slides up and Blue

appears. He perches on the windowsill and grins down at us. "Scary? That's not a very flattering description. Ah, well—I guess beauty is in the eye of the beholder."

"Let them go!" Vik demands angrily.

"Don't be alarmed," Blue says sweetly. "Your aunt and your sister haven't been harmed. I just thought you boys might need . . . a nudge, shall we say. I did make you an offer, after all."

"We don't need your help anymore!" Kenny shouts defiantly. "Jaxon can open the gate by himself."

My stomach lurches, and I clutch the crystal in my hand. I hope Kenny's right!

Blue just laughs. "Can he, now? I'd love to see him try. Why don't you boys come inside and we'll complete our transaction?"

For the first time, we notice that the factory doesn't have a front door. Blue sees our confusion and directs us around back. "You'll find the entrance at the base of the smokestack," he says, as if he's a nice neighbor inviting us over for tea.

We race over to the smokestack. Vik gets there first and grabs the knob of the door, but Kenny tugs at his arm.

"Wait—what if it's a trap?"

"We have to risk it," Vik insists breathlessly. "We can't just leave them up there."

"He's right," I say. "Blue probably will play a trick on us. We'll just have to outsmart him."

Jef nods approvingly and flies through the crack in the door. Vik pulls the door open wider and we file in. With the help of Jef's glowing wings, we see that there's a tunnel leading from the smokestack back to the factory. Jef burns bright as a candle, and we follow the red glow until we reach the end of the tunnel and enter a spacious warehouse. There's a wide staircase in the center of the room, and we cautiously head over to it.

"This place looks like a laboratory," Vik says.

He's right. There are a few wooden crates stacked against the walls, but two long tables run from the front to the back of the emporium, one on each side of the staircase. On top of both tables are glass beakers and test tubes full of colorful liquids. The blazing blue flames of Bunsen burners are causing some beakers to almost boil over. That could be dangerous, yet the air in the warehouse is fragrant—even a little intoxicating.

I notice that Jef has slid a finger under his nose to keep out the fumes. "Don't breathe too deeply," I warn my friends. "Who knows what kinds of potions Blue's got bubbling in those beakers."

"Welcome!"

Blue's voice booms from above, and we look up to find him at the top of the stairs. He begins to descend, his arms spread wide. "What do you think of my emporium?"

"*Your* emporium? What happened to Esmeralda?" Kenny asks.

Blue's smile vanishes. He bows his bald head and folds his hands together as if in prayer. "Sadly, she passed on, but dear Esmeralda was generous enough to leave her thriving business in my capable hands."

"What do you make here?" I ask, wishing I could

hide my curiosity and focus on finding Kavita and the dragon.

The grin returns to Blue's face. Shaking off his solemn pose, he bounces down the stairs and stands before us.

"What *don't* I make here?" Blue says with a bright laugh. "This, my dear boy, is the stuff of dreams." Blue proudly sweeps his arm over the table closest to us. "Potions, spells, curses, and hexes. Everything humans most desire—love, wealth, revenge, success. Put it in a bottle and slap on a price tag. Humans are so desperate to be happy, they'll buy just about anything." He winks at me and adds, "Plus, it's good PR, don't you think?"

"PR?"

Blue heaves an exasperated sigh. "Public relations! Try to keep up, kid. If magic is going to be restored to this world, the people have to be prepared. With every sale—and every satisfied customer—I'm generating goodwill for people like us and the creatures we represent."

"Sounds like a scam to me," Kenny mumbles.

Blue hears him, but his smile only widens. "Snake oil salesmen are disparaged by some but sought after by others. What's inside the bottle doesn't really matter—what matters is that people *believe*."

Blue's voice drops so low that the last word is barely a whisper. The Bunsen burner flames flicker, and the overhead lights dim for a moment. I shiver and take a step closer to Blue even though a part of me wants to run away—fast!

Vik breaks whatever spell I'm under by asking, "Where's my sister?"

"Upstairs, of course, with your aunt. Such a lovely woman. One of us, I think," Blue says, winking at me.

"I want to see them—now," Vik insists. He doesn't trust Blue and doesn't seem to care if it shows.

"Right this way," Blue says, holding out his arm.

Vik puts his foot on the first step, but I pull him back and say, "After you."

Blue nods and takes the stairs two at a time. We have to hustle to keep up with him and are panting by the time we reach the second floor. Blue isn't out of breath, though. There are two closed doors, one on either side of the landing. Neither door has a window, so there's no way to tell what's inside the rooms.

"You choose," Blue says coyly. "Door #1 or Door #2."

Vik looks from one door to the other and then calls out his sister's name.

We hear footsteps and then small fists pounding on Door #1. "Vikram? Are you there? Please, help me!"

Kavita's not my sister, but the sound of her crying behind that door nearly breaks *my* heart. Vik surges forward, but Kenny and I grab hold of his arms.

"I think it's a trick," I whisper in his ear. Jef nods vigorously and points at the opposite door. Vik strains against us but gradually calms down.

"Let my sister go," Vik tells Blue. "Kavita can be a total pain . . . but she's just a little girl."

"Sugar and spice and everything nice—that's what little girls are made of." Blue laughs, and the sound echoes eerily throughout the emporium. "Aren't you anxious to see her? Why don't you two have a little reunion and then we'll see what's behind Door #2?"

Blue grasps the knob and flings open the door on the left. Kavita runs out of the shadows and hurls herself at her brother. She sobs in his arms as Vik does his best to comfort her. "It's all right," he assures her. "You're safe now."

"I want to go home!" she cries.

"Soon, little one," Blue assures her with a careless pat on the head. "You wouldn't want to leave your dear aunt behind, would you? Let's see how she's doing."

Blue opens Door #2. There's no sound coming from the dark room, but Jef charges in and we follow the light from his wings. The room must be empty, because when

Kavita calls her aunt's name, her small voice fills the darkness.

"I'm over here, Kavita."

We follow her aunt's calm voice to the far corner of the room. Next to a window that reaches from the floor to the ceiling, we find the elderly woman standing opposite the dragon. The mauve sky is darker now, despite the absence of a sun. With Jef hovering overhead, there's enough light to see that Vik and Kavita's aunt is holding a red box in one hand. With the other she's feeding the dragon!

Before I can stop to think, I blurt out, "No!"

The dragon looks at me for a moment and then turns its attention back to the hand that's holding a small, round white cake—peda! I can't believe how much the dragon has grown since I saw it last. When I delivered its siblings to Sis, they were the size of mice. But this dragon is the size of a baby elephant—and it seems to grow larger with every bite of the sweet, creamy treat. I think of the small crystal in my pocket and wonder if it's powerful enough to send a creature that size back to the realm of magic. I'd have to find some type of container for it to travel in, and so far nothing I've seen inside the emporium is big enough to hold this growing dragon.

Kavita finally lets go of Vik's hand and runs over to her aunt. "Are you okay, Aunty?"

When Kavita starts crying again, the old woman makes a funny sound with her tongue. "Tut-tut-tut," she says before wiping away Kavita's tears with the hem of her sari. "Don't make a fuss, child. I'm fine. Mo and I were just having a snack."

"You aren't supposed to feed the dragon, Aunty," Vik says with an embarrassed glance in my direction.

Suddenly, Blue emerges from the shadows. "It would be cruel to let the poor creature starve, don't you think?"

"Ma said not to feed them anything sweet," I say.

Blue licks his lips. "That's because she had to carry three dragons to the realm of magic. She couldn't afford to have them any bigger than her thumb. But this magnificent creature isn't going anywhere." Blue walks over and strokes the dragon under its chin. It must like him, because it makes a sound similar to a cat's purring.

"Why is it so dark in here?" I ask.

Blue gives me a disappointed look. "You don't know much about dragons, do you, kid? Their eyes are very sensitive to light."

"Some reptiles have night vision," Vik tells me, "so I guess it makes sense that dragons would, too."

Dragons may have night vision, but we don't. It's hard to come up with a plan when I can't get a sense of the contents of the room. Blue isn't watching us too closely, which is good.

"I do love sugary things," Blue says. "Any peda left for me, Aunty?"

The old woman calmly pops the last cake into her own mouth before tossing the empty cardboard box on the floor. It slides to a stop at Blue's feet.

"That wasn't very nice," he says with a silly pout. "I've been such a hospitable host, and this is how you repay me?" Kavita glares at Blue, but her aunt refuses to even glance in his direction. "Well, perhaps it's time for you two to go home. You've served your purpose."

Kavita throws her arms around the dragon's neck. "I'm not leaving without Mo."

"I'm afraid that's not how gifts work, my dear. You gave the dragon to me, remember?"

"I didn't give you anything!" Kavita says with surprising ferociousness. Right now she is definitely scarier than the dragon! Mo, as she calls it, is nosing around in the empty box, clearly hoping for more peda.

Kavita flings her finger at Blue. "You stole Mo!"

Blue pretends to be shocked by Kavita's accusation.

"Stole? Well, ain't that the pot calling the kettle black!" he says huffily. "The only thief here is *you*! You took something that didn't belong to you—something very precious. Something *I* happen to need."

I tug at Vik's sleeve and pull him back into the shadows. "Keep Blue talking," I tell him. "I'm going to see if I can open the gate using the crystal."

Vik nods and steps back into the light cast by Jef's wings. "Why do you need a dragon? Haven't you already got one tattooed on your arm?"

Vik keeps his voice neutral enough to sound like he's genuinely curious, and Blue falls for it. I actually want to hear the answer to that question, but instead, I tap Kenny on the shoulder and draw him into the shadows with me.

"We need something big enough to cover the dragon," I whisper urgently.

Kenny looks around, but there isn't much we can see in the dark room. He searches the many pockets of his vest and pulls out a pen. With one quick click, a thin beam of light appears at the end. Kenny swings the pen flashlight around the spacious room. "Do you want a blanket?" he asks. "You can't hide something that big, Jax."

"We're not trying to hide it—we just need to contain

it," I explain. Kenny still looks confused, so I blurt out, "Piezoelectricity!"

I try not to sound as impatient as I feel. I'm so close! If I can just wrap the dragon up somehow, I might be able to open the gate and send it back where it belongs.

I answer Kenny's question before he can ask it. "If you crush a crystal, it will release an electrical charge. One time Ma used a crystal to move the transporter between realms. She said the charge and my own intentions steered the guardhouse where I wanted it to go. Maybe we can do that again now. Ma didn't have a guardhouse to travel in, so she used a hollow tree trunk."

"Tree trunk?" Kenny sounds impressed and doubtful at the same time. "No chance of that dragon fitting in one of those," he says, "even if there was a tree trunk lying around this emporium."

I hate to admit it, but Kenny's right. I glance over my shoulder to see what Blue's up to. Sounds like he's explaining the difference between a dragon and the sea serpent that's writhing up and down his arm.

"We also need to find a way to crush this crystal," I tell Kenny. I pull the rock from my pocket, and it sparkles when Kenny trains the flashlight on it. "Ma used a compression spell, but I don't know any spells yet. Maybe we could use something heavy instead."

129

Kenny glances around the big empty room. "I'm heavy," he says with a shrug. "What if I just stomp on it?"

A few hours ago, I was worried Kenny might stomp *me*! "That might work," I tell him. "I'll go over to that other room and see if I can find something to wrap the dragon in. Then I'll give you the signal, you'll smash the crystal, and we'll try to transport the dragon out of here." I don't let myself consider the possibility that our makeshift transporter could misfire and send the dragon to the Jurassic era instead of the realm of magic.

Kenny nods and holds out his fist. I bump it with my own, and he hands me his flashlight pen. "Thanks, Kenny," I say before turning back toward the door. Then I hear Blue call my name.

"Leaving so soon, Jax? You don't want to miss the show!"

I pocket the crystal and the flashlight before rejoining the group. "I was, er, just looking for the bathroom."

Blue raises one skeptical eyebrow. "It's downstairs. But worry about your bladder later—this remarkable woman has trained the dragon to do tricks!"

Vik and Kavita's aunt holds something high above her head, and even though the growing dragon now towers over her, it obeys her command and stands on its hind legs. She tosses the red-and-white-striped pepper-

130

mint into the air, and the dragon snaps it up. Next she holds another candy close to the floor. The dragon lies on its stomach and rolls onto its back, earning another treat.

"Quite impressive, don't you think?" Blue whispers confidentially, as if we're old friends.

"This isn't the circus," I say grouchily.

Blue sobers and studies me for a moment. "You have a good heart, Jaxon," he says finally. "I can see why Ma chose you for her apprentice."

"You know Ma?" I ask, somewhat surprised.

"Everyone knows Ma," he replies. Then he says, "We have something in common, you and I."

That seems unlikely, but I wait to hear what Blue has to say.

"We don't want to see these amazing creatures exploited. They should be allowed to live with dignity."

I hate to admit it, but I agree with Blue. Right now, performing tricks for treats, the dragon looks anything but dignified.

Vik's aunt is smiling like this little show really is amusing. Then her smile changes. I'm not sure how, but I know it's different. She's about to do something—I can tell. If Blue knows what's coming, he doesn't let on.

"Speak," says the old woman.

The dragon tilts its head to one side and studies her for a moment. Then its eyes fix on the candy she's holding between her finger and thumb.

"Speak." The old woman's voice is lower this time, and softer. But the dragon obeys. The floor shakes as it thumps its plated tail upon the wooden boards. Then it tilts its head back and utters a single wail.

The hairs on the back on my neck stand up. I glance around the room and notice that everyone seems to be cringing. The dragon's voice has the same effect as nails being drawn across a chalkboard. Instead of flinging the candy into the dragon's mouth, Aunty repeats her command.

"Speak!"

Again the dragon thumps its tail on the floor three times. Then it rears up on its hind legs, opens its fanged jaws, and shrieks. Kavita flies into her brother's arms. Kenny clamps his hands over his ears. I fall forward onto my hands and knees—and that's when I drop the crystal.

It rolls across the wooden floorboards. Kenny spots it and lunges at the crystal. He just means to stop it from rolling into the shadows, but his giant foot lands on top of it instead. The pressure of his weight on the crystal releases a blinding flash of light that sends the dragon into a fit. It shrieks and slams its tail into the window this time, shattering the glass. Blue tries to soothe the frantic creature, but Aunty just watches the spectacle with a small smile on her lips. When the dragon finally quiets, another sound fills the room. Actually, we feel the rumble before we hear it.

"What's happening?" Kenny asks, gingerly removing his foot to inspect the crystal. It glows brightly and remains intact. "Did it work?" Kenny asks hopefully.

I shake my head and put the crystal back in my pocket. The dragon is just where we left it, which means the gate didn't open—I think. But in my gut, I feel like the crystal *did* work. Something's coming— something big!

12

JAXON

The building starts to shake, throwing us all off balance.

Vik looks at me over his sister's head. He silently mouths the word "Earthquake?"

Intuition tells me it's not an earthquake. I shake my head, and Vik holds his sister a bit tighter. I guess I should be worried, but right now I feel strangely calm.

Blue looks anything but calm! With all his tattoos it's hard to tell, but I think he must feel queasy because he looks more green than blue. He backs away from the dragon, his hands held up in surrender. "Well played, madam. That was very clever indeed."

It takes me a few seconds to realize that he's talking to Aunty. She's still smiling and calmly feeding peppermints to the dragon. I go over to what's left of the window and look up at the smokestack. It's starting to wobble. Kenny joins me and panics when the quaking intensifies.

"Look out!" he cries, covering his head with his arms. Kavita screams, but the tower doesn't topple. Instead, its bricks loosen and expand, rapidly spinning around and around like an upside-down tornado. The dizzying effect conceals the fact that something is growing inside—and emerging from—the smokestack!

"*That's* the gate," I whisper to myself. Suddenly, everything makes sense. Vik's aunt must have known what would happen when the baby dragon's cries reached its mother's ears. . . .

All of a sudden, my ears pop, and the roof of the emporium flips open like the hinged lid of the mint tin. The mauve sky has darkened, and the moon floats above us like a pearl in a pool of ink. I jump at the sound of thunder and then realize it's the swirling bricks from the disassembled smokestack that are falling to the ground, raising an immense cloud of dust. A strong gust of wind clears the air, and a monstrous beast looms above us.

I blink, and then I blink again. I can hardly believe my eyes! Unlike our happily purring baby dragon, this adult one looks truly menacing. Yet something about the orange eyes of the black-scaled, black-winged dragon looks familiar. It points its snout at the sky, and fire spews from its mouth like lava from a volcano. Sparks rain down on us as the dragon grips the roofless walls of the emporium with its sharp talons and lowers its horned head.

For just a second, the dragon shimmers like a hologram, and I understand why it looks familiar. When it's not a dragon, it's a tall, haughty woman with a long black braid—it's Sis! She wavers like a flame—a giant, angry woman in one moment and a fierce dragon in the next. I'm not sure which one's scarier!

Blue tries to act brave, but one thunderous roar from Sis makes every single one of us tremble. Even the creatures tattooed onto Blue's body flee from Sis and disappear from sight under his clothes. Only Jef has the courage to approach the dragon. The fairy flies up into the sky, whispers something in Sis's ear, and then perches on one of her horns, as if awaiting orders.

The dragon peers into the emporium and blows hot air out of her nostrils. We cluster together, leaving Blue on his own to confront Sis. When she speaks in her dragon form, her voice is a low rumble.

"You were warned," Sis growls.

Blue retreats until his back is against the wall. "I've done nothing wrong!" he cries, but the desperation in his voice reveals his guilt.

"Liar!" Sis's forked tongue waggles at Blue from

between massive fangs. "Those creatures do not belong to you."

Having the wall at his back seems to lend Blue some courage. He straightens and shouts back, "They're not yours, either!" Under his breath he mutters, "You claim everything for yourself. . . ."

Sis hears him and brings her snout even closer to Blue's face. "I am charged with protecting these creatures. They are not safe in this world."

"And whose fault is that?" Blue demands, defiant despite being trapped in a corner by the dragon's massive head. "They have a right to be here—this is their world, too! But *you* wouldn't fight for them. *You* surrendered and retreated to the other realm, insisting that everyone go along with you. *You* never gave *them* a choice!"

Sis rears up once more, and I expect to see fire shoot out of her mouth, but instead she twirls gracefully in the star-filled sky and reappears inside the emporium in her usual human form. She stands before Blue, still proud but less menacing, with Jef perched on her shoulder.

"You claim to love them, and yet you would put these creatures in harm's way for the sake of an experiment that you know will fail. Why doesn't their safety matter as much to you as it does to me, I wonder?"

Blue seems to relax a bit now that Sis is human once

more. He takes a step away from the wall and tries to reason with her as an equal. "Because life is filled with risk, Sis. And yes—I would risk losing every last one of my special friends in order to see them free to live how and where they want to once more."

I know it's the wrong thing to do, but I can't keep quiet anymore. I step forward and clear my throat. "Excuse me for interrupting but . . . why can't Blue's 'guests' stay here, Sis? If magic was part of this world once, can't it be that way again?"

Sis turns her head and glares at me. "Keep quiet, boy," she says with a dismissive wave of her hand. "This does not concern you."

Mama taught me never to talk back to a grown-up, but I forget about my home training for the moment. "Actually, it does concern me because I'm Ma's apprentice and it's my job to bring the last dragon back to the realm of magic."

"That's right!" Blue cries, looking past Sis to the rest of us. "You can't keep making executive decisions. I say we take a vote." Blue's hand shoots toward the sky. "How many people want to see magic restored to this world?"

I glance around the roofless room. Like me, everyone else has their hand up. Vindicated, Blue laughs and steps around Sis to address us.

"Ha—I knew it! That's how decisions ought to be made. Not by one person. Not by"—he points his finger at Sis and adds—"a tyrant."

Jef flies straight at Blue and makes a sound like a hissing cat. Then, as if feeling a tug on his invisible leash, Jef returns to Sis.

"I see," Sis says solemnly, turning to face us. "And what will you do when every single one of these creatures is harvested for its . . . special properties?" Sis pauses briefly and then goes on, her voice rising in volume. "Which one of you will dedicate your life to preserving theirs?"

We look at one another and then down at the floor. Kavita inches closer to Mo and strokes its neck gently. "I tried to take good care of Mo, but . . ."

Kavita has made some bad choices that caused a lot of problems for a lot of people, but she's just a little kid. Sis shows no sympathy, however, and looms over her. "But you failed because you are ignorant of what an infant dragon needs. And then you delivered the dragon to this . . . fool!"

Kavita looks like she wants to start bawling, but she stubbornly refuses to crack under Sis's glare. "He took Mo from us," she says weakly.

"Proving you are unable—and unfit—to care for something so precious."

"The child meant no harm," Aunty says, putting her arm around Kavita. "We did what we could to make amends."

Sis appraises the old woman and shows her a bit more respect. "Yes, you were right to summon me. But do you think I can come to this world every time one of my wards is in danger? They must return with me—all of them. Now."

Sis holds one hand palm up in front of herself. Blue starts to stammer as he backs up against the wall once more. "N-no—no, you can't—you wouldn't . . . you promised!"

The tiniest smile touches Sis's lips. With her other hand, she points at the floor at Blue's feet. Then she flips that hand and slowly pulls it toward her as it moves up Blue's quaking body. Even though he is powerless to stop Sis, Blue wraps his arms around himself and turns away. We see movement beneath his clothing and hear a faint clamor as Sis extracts the creatures tattooed on Blue's skin. One by one the mermaid, parrot, sea serpent, unicorn, and others peel off and float toward Sis. Still in miniature, the creatures huddle together and are soon encased in a clear sphere that forms above Sis's outstretched palm.

When the last fairy presses a kiss into Blue's cheek

before heeding the summons, the miserable man sinks to the floor. His sobs make my own throat ache, and I truly feel sorry for Blue.

"I was going to free them," he whimpers.

Sis seals the sphere before lifting it above her head and using her palm to gently push it over the wall of the emporium. It floats in the night sky for a moment before dropping toward the pile of bricks that ring the base of the smokestack. Dark hands reach out of the shadows to catch the sphere. I peer into the shadows and think I catch a glimpse of a tall man with a gray beard.

"Trub!" I cry, thrilled to see my grandfather.

He salutes me, and his gold tooth gleams in the

moonlight. Then he turns his attention back to the sphere. Holding it between his palms, Trub touches his forehead to the glowing, pulsing orb. I can't hear what he's saying, but after a few seconds, he releases the sphere and it gets sucked into the ground. The creatures have passed through the gate and are on their way back to the realm of magic.

Blue's pitiful sobs bring my attention back inside the emporium. "Did you hear that? Did you hear their lament? No, of course not. You learned to shut your ears a long time ago—your heart, too."

Blue slumps against the wall but turns enough to fling a hand out and point accusingly at Sis. He looks at me and asks, "Did you know that about Sis? She's an expert at looking the other way. The slave trade flourished right beneath her nose. People—*your* people— were shackled and sold and shipped across the sea, and Sis watched it happen. She *let* it happen."

Aunty gasps and holds the hem of her sari to her mouth. I swallow hard and feel my cheeks burn the way they always do whenever my social studies teacher talks about slavery with her eyes trained on me.

Blue grins and looks a bit like his old playful self. Mischief makes his gray eyes gleam. "Tell me, Jaxon, what would the world be like without the specter of slavery?" Then he lowers his voice and adds, "What has your world been like without your father, Jax?"

My heart stops for just a second. I take a deep breath to start it beating again and say, "Leave my dad out of this."

Blue keeps his eyes locked on mine. He presses his pale hands against the wall and claws at the bricks to help him stand. "It's been almost two years. You must wonder sometimes . . . did he really have to die?"

I blink quickly to stop the tears from filling up my eyes. I know Blue's playing some sort of game, but I can't seem to keep myself from being drawn in. "Bad things happen," I tell him, just as Mama told me that terrible night. "There's nothing we can do about that."

"There's nothing *you* can do. But *she* could."

"More lies!" Sis snarls, folding her arms across her chest. Jef mimics the gesture, and both glare at Blue with obvious disdain.

Blue flinches and pushes himself away from the wall. He staggers forward, and I rush to catch him when it seems he might fall. Blue grasps my shoulders and looks into my eyes. "I'm telling you the truth, Jax. Ask her! Ask her why she won't use her power to end the suffering in our world."

Sis turns away, as if she can't be bothered to entertain such a ridiculous question. But suddenly, I really want to know—could magic make our world a better place? Could Sis have saved my dad?

"Could you do that, Sis?"

Jef leaves Sis's shoulder and flies up to my face. The fairy holds up one hand and signals for me to stop. Kenny steps forward and speaks on my behalf. "He needs to know, Jef. Jax has been through a lot. Sis owes him an answer, don't you think?"

Jef looks from Kenny, to me, and then spins to face Sis. I can't tell what passes between them, but it seems like Jef is pleading with his boss. Sis finally draws closer. Blue's grip on my shoulders loosens, and he quietly slinks into the shadows.

Sis towers over me, her dark eyes hard and cruel. "Tell me, boy, who is responsible for the suffering in your world? The famines, the wars, the many diseases that have no known cure?"

I think for a moment. Sis has taken Blue's place, but I still feel like I'm being asked to play a game. "We are, I guess. I mean, some humans are to blame—the leaders of our countries." My voice goes up at the end, which makes my answer sound more like a question.

Sis nods. "Then why should the creatures in my care solve problems they haven't created?" I have no answer for that, and Sis doesn't give me time to think of one. "How do you think this fool makes his potions?" she asks me. "He siphons the magical abilities of his so-called guests."

"I took no more than I needed!" Blue calls weakly from the shadows. "My guests were happy to share their gifts with me and my clients."

Sis puts a finger to my chin and turns my head so I am facing her once more. "Our worlds can only coexist if there is balance—life and death, loss and gain. If anyone were to interfere and upset that balance, there would be a price to pay in your realm and in mine."

"But innocent people are paying a price right now," I insist. "Good people die for no reason. That's not fair!"

For just a moment, I think I see a flicker of sympathy in Sis's dark eyes. She removes the sharp fingernail pressing into my chin and instead cups my cheek with her surprisingly soft palm.

"Suffering is what makes you human, Jax. Without scarcity and loss, there would be no reason to develop gratitude for abundance. Without pain, you would never appreciate moments of joy. If there is imbalance in your world, that is not—that cannot be—my concern. I am a guardian of the realm of magic. Your people have chosen fools as leaders. If you want change, you must hold them accountable—or become a leader yourself."

"Who would follow me?" I mumble pathetically.

I'd almost forgotten Vik and Kenny are still in the room. Vik's confident voice startles me.

"We would!" he says.

"We've been following you all day," Kenny adds, "and I've seen some amazing things: dragons, fairies. . . ." Kenny pauses to gaze reverently up at Sis. He quietly adds, "Plus, I never met a queen before."

Sis frowns. "I am no queen, boy. I am a guardian. You," Sis says, turning my head once more, "were entrusted with a mission. You failed." She takes a step back and glances out the window at the pile of rubble behind the emporium. "I could have retrieved the lost dragon myself, but I gave you a chance to put things right. Why?"

You failed. Those two words sting even though they're true. I feel my cheeks burn and look at the floor so Sis can't see my shame. "I don't know," I mumble. "Maybe you felt sorry for me?"

Sis raises her voice, compelling me to look her in the eye. I can't tell if it's magic or just my fear, but Sis appears to grow taller with each word.

"Listen closely, boy. I gave you a second chance so that you could prove your worth—not just to me, but to yourself. You accepted the opportunity to redeem yourself, and you have done so admirably."

My cheeks burn some more, but this time, it's with pride.

Sis looms over me. "I am sorry you lost your father," she says with genuine sympathy, "but we must all face trials in our lives. Without challenges, we would never know our capacity for courage, compassion, and forgiveness." Sis glares at the shivering heap of limbs that Blue has become. "Revenge is a temptation we must resist. Even the lowest amongst us can be redeemed."

Jef whispers in her ear, and Sis looks up at the moon. "My time here is at an end," she says with a weary sigh. "You faced these challenges because of your love for Ma. She is also dear to me. Take this."

From the folds of her dress, Sis pulls a small, carved bottle. I step forward to accept it. "What's this?" I ask.

"A true potion—nothing like the ones concocted downstairs by that fool. Three drops in a glass of water will rouse her. Do it soon, before the moon wanes."

"Thank you, Sis," I say, humbled by the trust she has placed in me.

"Farewell, Jaxon," Sis says. She takes a moment to look at my friends as well. "Your loyalty will be rewarded." Then she turns to the dragon, which has continued to grow and is now nearly as big as an adult elephant. "Time to go home, little one," Sis says with affection and even a hint of a smile. The dragon rears up on its hind legs and looks at her quizzically. Sis points at the creature and draws a circle around it once, twice, and by the third time another elastic sphere has formed. Unlike Blue's tattoos, however, the dragon doesn't accept its fate. It whines and claws against the sphere, but to no avail.

Kavita sniffles and holds out a hand to the confused creature. "I'll never forget you, Mo," she says tearfully.

Sis touches the sphere with her hand, and the dragon calms somewhat. Then she effortlessly lifts it into the sky and pushes it over the emporium wall. Trub is ready to catch the glistening sphere, and he performs the same ritual before sending it through the gate.

I sigh with relief. It didn't happen the way I thought it would, but the last dragon is finally on its way home. I wish Ma were here so she could know I played a small part in fulfilling her final mission.

"Are you ready?"

The sound of Sis's voice brings me back to the present. I look at her outstretched hand and then realize she's not offering it to me. Aunty steps forward and places her small, wrinkled hand in Sis's.

"Aunty, no!" Kavita cries. Vik grabs his sister before she can fling herself at the elderly woman.

"I want to go home, child," Aunty explains. "This may be as close as I will ever get to finding a place where I belong."

That seems to make sense to Kavita, because she nods and leans against her brother. Their aunt smiles and places a hand on each of their bowed heads. "I've found my purpose," she says with pride. "I will take good care of Mo. Don't worry about either of us. Can you do something for me, Kavita?"

Through her tears, Kavita says, "Yes, Aunty— anything."

"The quilt on my bed is precious to me. You'll take good care of it, won't you?"

Kavita nods and gives her aunt one last hug before wrapping her arms around Vik.

Jef flies over to Kenny and silently places a tiny hand on his rosy cheek. Then Jef zips back to Sis, who draws another circle. As the sphere closes around them, I hear the crackle of electricity. Sis points upward this time, and we watch as they rise into the sky. Sis steers them to the mound of bricks circling the gate. She holds Aunty close, nods at Trub, and then they vanish as the gate opens and sucks them out of our world.

13

JAXON

The roof flips shut with a loud boom, leaving us in darkness. Without Jef's wings to guide us, we fumble in the darkness until I pull out Kenny's flashlight. Even then, when we turn to leave, we nearly trip over Blue. He lies sprawled on the floor, his bare arms trembling still.

"What should we do?" I ask my friends.

"What *can* we do?" Kenny counters.

"There's only one way to find out," Vik says sensibly.

I go over and tap Blue on the shoulder. "Do you need help?"

To my surprise, he barks, "No!" That's when I realize he's shaking with rage and not from the cold.

"Go away, you rotten brats! You've ruined everything—everything!"

Kenny tugs at my arm. "Forget this jerk. Let's go home."

We find our way back to the landing and have almost reached the bottom of the stairs when we hear Blue's voice once more.

He stands on the top step, sneering at us. "It isn't over, you know. No matter how many times Sis demotes me, no matter how many times she seals a gate—I always find a way to link the realms. And I'm not the only one Sis has to worry about."

Kenny tries to pull me along, but something in Blue's tone makes me determined to face him. I frown and demand, "What's that supposed to mean?"

Blue just sneers at me. "Ask Ma—she'll tell you. There's a reason we formed a union. I can file another grievance against Sis or . . ."

"Or what?"

Blue turns to go. Over his shoulder he says, "This isn't over. I have allies, too! You'll be seeing me again, kid."

That sounds like a threat. I might have felt afraid, but a friendly, familiar voice chases all my fears away.

"Don't listen to that windbag, Jaxon. He's just bitter because he got outsmarted—again."

Blue's lip curls with disdain at the sight of Trub. I race over and throw my arms around my granddad. He staggers a bit and pulls my head back gently with his hand. "Thought I'd forgotten about you?"

I hate to admit it, but when I nod, Trub just smiles.

"I promised you'd see me again. I searched high and low for a working transporter, but those sick little dragons have everything shut down. So I bided my time and kept an eye on Sis—I had a feeling she'd be crossing over to collect what was hers. When she opened the last gate, I offered my services and tagged along."

"I'm glad you were there. Blue got me so mixed up . . . there were times when I didn't know what to think."

"You listened to your heart. That's what it means to work in these strange, wonderful worlds. You don't just have to believe in magic—you have to believe in yourself."

"It helps to have friends who've got your back." I'm talking to Trub, but I'm looking at Vik, Kavita, and Kenny.

"You make a good team," Trub admits. "I'd like to thank all of you for helping out my grandson." Trub has already met Vik and his sister, so he shakes hands with just Kenny.

I glance upstairs in time to see Blue disappear behind Door #1. Without his "guests," he looks pretty lonely, yet Blue did say he had "allies." Are there really more people who are willing to defy Sis?

"What will happen to Blue now?" I ask as Trub leads us out of the emporium.

He just gives my shoulder a squeeze and pushes me ahead of him as we pass through the dark tunnel. When we emerge, the smokestack stands just as it was when we first arrived. The empty lots are fenced once more, and graffiti covers the brick walls of the spice factory.

"You all go ahead. I got one last job to finish," Trub says.

As soon as we reach the street, Trub flares the fingers of his left hand. Then he makes a tight fist with the same hand, and we watch in awe as the entrance at the base of the smokestack is once more sealed tight with cement blocks.

"What do we do now?" Kenny asks.

"I have to give Ma a dose of this tincture," I say, suddenly sad to be parting from my friends. "You guys have been so amazing—I never could have done this without you."

Kavita is still weeping softly, her face turned into her brother's chest. Vik gives her a squeeze and tries to reassure her.

"It's what Aunty wanted, Kavi. You want her to be happy, right?" When Kavita nods, Vik takes hold of her hand. "Let's go. Mummy and Papa will be worried about us. And I want to tell them how brave you were today."

As they turn to go, Kavita looks back over her shoulder. "We made things right, Jax," she says quietly.

I nod and wave as they head down the street. Kenny coughs and crosses his arms over his chest. Before this adventure, I would have thought that meant Kenny was about to clobber someone. But now I know that's what he does when he's not sure what to say.

"Thanks for your help, Kenny. You got more than you bargained for when you offered to help us open that mint tin!"

Kenny smiles shyly and looks at his feet. "I guess I'll tell my mom we finished our project for school."

"Do you have a partner for the science fair?"

Kenny shakes his head and looks down the block. The streetlights have come on, but I can still see the pink glow of his cheeks. "I never have a partner. It's easier to just work on my own."

"Why don't we ask Mr. Iqbal if we can work as a trio?"

Kenny brings his eyes back to mine. "Really?"

I nod. "Sure. You, me, and Vik—we make a pretty good team. Don't you think?"

Kenny nods and unfolds his arms. "Wait till I tell my mom—she'll be so excited! We really are friends now, right?"

"Of course! Maybe Vik and I can come over later this week. We can help your mom experiment until she makes a decent kale smoothie."

Kenny laughs and shoves his hands in his pockets. They're empty, and that wipes the smile off his freckled face. "Do you think we'll ever see Jef again?"

I finger the small bottle in my own pocket. Once Ma gets better, she'll retire and head back to the realm of magic. I wonder if Sis will come back to collect her. If she does, Jef might tag along. "It's hard to say, Kenny. But Jef's in a beautiful place and all of his friends are there. Well, not all of them."

Kenny smiles and pulls his hands out of his pockets. "I better head home. You coming?"

"You go ahead," I tell him. "I just need to make one quick stop."

Kenny waves as he heads down the block.

Whistling softly, my granddad comes out of the shadows. He brushes dust off his clothes and nods at me. "I think that about does it. No one would ever know we had quite a dustup here a short while ago. Ready?"

I look up at the smokestack and think about the lost gate. We only have this world now. "I need to find a ghost," I say cryptically.

Trub frowns but doesn't ask me to explain. "Want me to come with you?" he asks.

I shake my head. "You go catch up with Mama. I need to do this on my own."

Trub nods and gives my shoulder a squeeze. "You're a brave boy, Jax. If your daddy were here today, he'd be mighty proud of you. I know I am. Now I need to borrow some of your courage and go apologize to your mama. Think she'll hear me out?"

"Definitely . . . I mean, probably."

Trub takes a deep breath. He's seen a lot of wild stuff in the realm of magic, but facing his grown daughter has got Trub shook.

I try to help him out. "It's all in the delivery, right? If you start with a sincere apology for walking out on her all those years ago, Mama will let you in." I don't specify whether I mean into the apartment or into her life.

"Right. Thanks for the advice, Jax. I'll see you soon," Trub says before walking toward Ma's apartment. I take a deep breath and head over to Flatbush Avenue. It's time for me to stop hiding from the past, too.

My heart pounds hard until I reach the block where it happened. Then I find myself feeling surprisingly calm. When I find the storefront, there are no signs of damage. The SUV that plowed into my father took out the store's display window, but there's no proof of that now. People hurry by on the bustling avenue, and no one stops to wonder why a boy like me is standing in front of a women's clothing boutique. No one would know that my father's life ended here. No one would know from looking at me that I am a witch's apprentice with a magical potion in my pocket. I pull the small bottle out of my pocket and remember what Sis said. Once Ma has recovered, she'll leave me, too. But I can't let my selfish heart stop me from doing what's right. I turn and head back up Flatbush Avenue. It's time to go home.

When I reach Ma's floor, I put my ear to the door to hear what's going on inside. Mama and Trub are talking—not yelling—which is good.

"How'd Jax do today?" Mama asks.

"Just fine," Trub replies with pride. "Boy's got a knack for it."

"Well, he didn't get it from me," Mama says with a laugh. "Guess he must take after you."

There's a short pause, and then my granddad asks, "That all right with you—Jax joining the family business, so to speak?"

I hold my breath and wait for Mama to respond.

"Can't really stop him, can I?"

Trub chuckles. "Probably not. Jax is pretty determined—and he's loyal to Ma. He knows she can't work on her own anymore. But he sure would like to have your approval, Alicia."

Mama sighs. "You and Ma will look out for him?"

"Of course!" Trub replies, but Mama's not convinced.

"Promise me, Daddy—promise me this time you'll put family first."

Trub says nothing for a long moment. Finally, he says, "I'm a lot older now—and at least a little bit wiser. I promise I'll do right by both of you, Alicia."

I decide that's my cue to turn the key and let myself into the apartment. Mama rushes over to me. Brushing tears from her eyes, she folds me in her arms and then holds me at arm's length to inspect me.

"Jaxon—are you all right?"

I step in close and give Mama another hug. I peek around her arm and see my granddad sitting in the living room.

I look up at my mother and say, "I'm fine, Mama. How 'bout you?"

Mama smiles as she wipes her tears away. "I'm good, baby. Your grandfather and I were just . . . talking. Are you hungry? I could make us some dinner or we could order in, if you like."

"Maybe Trub could fix something for us to eat."

Trub clears his throat and gets to his feet. "There's nothing I'd like more than to cook for my family." He looks at Mama and humbly adds, "If that's all right with you, Alicia."

"It's Ma's kitchen, but I'm sure she wouldn't mind. I picked up some groceries on the way home from work."

Trub heads for the kitchen and Mama pulls me along, but I hang back. "I need to check on Ma," I tell her. Mama nods and disappears down the long hallway.

I pull the small, carved bottle from my pocket. I've repeated Sis's instructions over and over in my head. I knock before entering Ma's room even though I know she won't hear me. She's slumped against the pillows we stacked under her head. I left Ma's purse on the chair beside her bed, but now it's tucked under her arm. Could Ma have woken up while I was out? She won't wake up again unless I give her this medicine, so I get to work.

There's a glass of water on the nightstand. The stopper pops loudly when I pull it out of the bottle. I take a quick sniff, but whatever's inside the bottle is odorless. I tip the bottle over the glass and carefully let three drops fall into the water. The potion is black, and within seconds the water in the glass starts to fizz. Before the frothy liquid can spill over the top, the bubbling stops and the water grows as thick as tar.

Mama gave me a pack of reusable straws for my birthday. I always carry one in my book bag so I don't have to use plastic straws when I'm eating out. I find

the metal straw and, with a little effort, shove it into the dark sludge. I'm not sure how Ma's going to suck that up a straw, but I hope her lips are as strong as Jef's. I take a portable spoon out of my bag as well, just in case.

Turns out I don't need it, though, because as soon as I place the glass in front of Ma's face, her nose starts to twitch. I can't smell anything, but I guess Ma's senses are sharper than mine. Her eyes remain closed, but she stops snoring and her lips part. Then a sound comes from somewhere deep inside Ma—not a word but a plea. I place the straw between her lips and hold my breath.

Nothing happens. I exhale and sink onto the bed, disappointed. I reach for the spoon I set on the nightstand and accidentally tug the straw from between Ma's lips. To my surprise, she lets out an angry groan. Then Ma's eyes fly open!

"Ma!" I cry. "Hurry—drink this. All of it!"

I push the straw between her lips once more, and with one strong slurp, Ma sucks every bit of the black sludge out of the glass. Then her eyes close and she sinks back against the stack of pillows. I wait breathlessly to see what will happen next. I hear Mama and Trub coming down the hall, and soon they're standing behind me. Mama puts her hand on my shoulder, and Trub puts his arm around Mama.

"She's waking up!" I tell them.

Mama gives my shoulder a squeeze. "Why don't you come have something to eat, Jaxon?"

I grab hold of Ma's hands. "I can't leave her now—she just woke up." I look over my shoulder and see Mama exchanging a doubtful glance with Trub. "It happened—really! I gave Ma the medicine Sis gave me. She sucked it out of the glass—look." But the glass is empty, and there's no trace of the tar-like substance.

I frown and stare at Ma, silently willing her to wake up.

"Maybe it just takes a little time for the medicine to kick in," Trub says. "Come have some supper, Jax."

I shake my head. "You two go ahead. I'm staying here with Ma."

Mama takes her hand off my shoulder. But instead of walking away, she sits down beside me. Trub eases himself into the chair next to Ma's bed. When I feel Mama's hand rubbing my back, a few tears spill down my cheek. I'm not sad, though—I'm proud. This is my family. Sure, we're different from other families. Ma's a witch, and I'm her apprentice. Mama's a widow, and Trub's a reformed thief. We've all made mistakes—big and small—but we stick together because that's what you do when you love someone.

Another minute goes by. Ma's hands are cold, so I rub them to warm them up. Then I stop because I can feel Ma's fingers moving on their own. She tries to pull her hands away from mine, but I'm not ready to let go.

"Ma? Can you hear me? We're all here, Ma. You're not alone."

Ma licks her lips and croaks, "You trying to break my hands, boy? I already got arthritis—I don't need you cracking every bone. Turn me loose!"

I grin and do as I'm told. Ma sounds just like her usual grouchy self!

She opens her eyes and looks over at Trub. He nods at her and says, "Welcome back, Ma. You've been missed."

Ma grunts and looks past me at Mama. "Guess you're fixing to say, 'I told you so.'"

Mama actually laughs. "I never could have predicted any of this," she says, "but I'm glad you're all right."

"You *are* all right, aren't you, Ma?" I ask.

Ma doesn't respond, and she still won't look at me. Instead, she sends Mama and Trub away. "I appreciate your concern, but I need a moment alone with my apprentice."

Mama gives me a kiss on the cheek. "Come join us in the kitchen when you're done," she says.

"Can I fix you a plate, Ma?" Trub asks as he gets to his feet.

"No appetite yet," she says. "Go on and break bread with your daughter. It's about time."

Trub nods. "I guess you and Jax got some catching up to do."

When Ma doesn't respond, Trub winks at me and ducks out the door. Soon Ma and I are alone in her room.

For a long while, Ma doesn't say anything. She just rummages through her purse, muttering softly under her breath.

I don't understand why Ma wanted to be alone with me if she's not going to speak. Finally, I clear my throat to get her attention. "Are you mad at me, Ma?" I ask timidly.

Ma stops digging in her purse and glares at me. "Why would I be mad at you?"

I shrug and look at the floor. "Because all of this is my fault! Leaving one dragon behind made you sick, and the two other dragons suffered, too."

"They weren't in any real danger, not with Sis watching over them. Those poor creatures were just pining for their sibling. Now their family is reunited."

"Like ours," I say.

Ma takes a tube out of her purse and squeezes some ointment onto her palm. She rubs it into her hands, and soon the smell of menthol fills the room. "I'm old, Jax," Ma says finally. "My bones are weary."

"You slept a really long time," I remind her.

Ma just sighs and shakes her head. "Not long enough. Besides, that was a waking dream. I wasn't really asleep—just trapped in a dream state."

Ma wasn't really asleep? Could've fooled me. "You were snoring," I tell her.

"I'm sure I was. My body was in sleep mode, but my mind was wide awake. Did you really think I'd let my apprentice go through all of that alone?"

I frown. "You mean . . . you were with me?"

Ma nods. "Sis, too. That's why she insisted on sending that butterfly back to Brooklyn with us."

"So Jef was a spy!"

"More of a proxy—sort of like a substitute teacher," Ma corrects me. "You and I never had time to establish a psychic connection, but I did the best I could to track you."

Suddenly, it starts to make sense. "When we were at the factory, I felt like I heard your voice. I thought it was just a memory. You really were talking to me?"

"Well, Jax, you're no robot—I couldn't tell you what to do. But I did try to guide you."

I feel my grin stretching from ear to ear. "We make a good team, right?"

Ma tries to smile at me, but she still looks sad. "You're a real capable apprentice, Jax. I wish I had the strength to give you the training you deserve."

My grin disappears. "So you're still going to retire?" I ask.

"Have to, Jax. It's time."

"But . . . Sis went back without you. She left you behind."

Ma nods. "She's given me a bit more time to put my

affairs in order. I wish I could get you a train ticket and send you off to some castle, but this ain't England—or Hollywood. This is Brooklyn. You're gonna have to hustle if you want to make this work."

"Hustle?"

"I'll handle as much of your training as I can, but I'm going to need you to do the rest. That means doing what you've done today—reaching out to the community."

"I trusted Blue. I didn't want to, but . . ."

"Blue's a trickster. But I daresay you learned something from your encounter with him. You found some of the creatures who are our allies, and you already know L. Roy. Trub won't ever steer you wrong. And I ain't the only witch in this city. I'll fill in some of the gaps myself and introduce you to some of the folks in my coven. How's that sound?"

I pretend to think for a moment, even though there's nothing I'd like more. Then I grin and say, "Sounds good to me, Ma."

"That's settled, then," Ma replies. "Now—go get me a beer! You didn't drink all of it, did you?"

I laugh and get to my feet. "I thought about it. But there was just one bottle left, and I knew you'd be thirsty when you woke up."

Ma's face gets softer somehow. "You always believed I'd come back, huh? The young are natural optimists, I suppose. You're wise for your years, Jax. I probably don't have to tell you that sometimes in this line of work—in life generally—you don't get a happy ending."

"I know. But we got one today! You're awake again, and the dragon is back in the realm of magic with its siblings. It's time to celebrate!"

Ma slaps her thigh and laughs. "Then let's get this party started, boy! Bring me my beer!"

ACKNOWLEDGMENTS

It takes a village to write a novel, and I'm grateful for the many readers, writers, teachers, scholars, parents, and librarians who help me tell stories that matter to our community. When I learned about the Siddis, my friend Dr. Rosamond S. King told me about Dr. Sarah Khan, cofounder of the Siddi Women's Quilting Cooperative. I wrote a kawandi quilt into *The Dragon Thief* and later purchased a beautiful one for myself; you can support the Siddi community by doing the same (africanquiltsofindia.com). As a child, I never knew about Africans in India, and I hope Aunty piques the interest of a new generation of readers. I'd like to thank Dr. Soniya Munshi, who answered countless questions and helped ensure a respectful and accurate depiction of the Patel family. Purvi Shah gave me great advice before I even started writing *The Dragon Thief,* and I appreciated having her expert eyes on the manuscript as well. I'm grateful for the advice on gender I received from

Matthew Smith, which helped us rethink our fairy's identity.

I pride myself on meeting deadlines, but I was late turning in this manuscript! Christmas was coming, and I had a bad cold—I finally just gave up and hit send. I'd like to thank my editor, Diane Landolf, for being so patient and for asking thoughtful questions that made the story stronger. In publishing, it helps to know you've got someone in your corner, and I know I'm lucky to have an editor and an agent who let me take risks in my writing. I'm grateful that Jennifer Laughran found a good home for my Brooklyn-born dragons.

I no longer live in Brooklyn, but I managed to stay in that beautiful neighborhood for eleven years because my friend Dorothy kindly allowed me to sublet her condo. I live in Philadelphia now, and I'm sure I'll find magic here, too. Wherever I am, I'll continue to write about Black magic, Black history, and the way community connects us all.